RAIDER LEAVES A MESSAGE

The dude grabbed the bottle by its neck and swung it hard against Raider's forehead. The glass shattered and blood streamed down Raider's face. The Pinkerton never blinked, he did not move a muscle—only stared at the man who had hit him. This kind of unnerved the dude, who was left holding the jagged bottle neck.

Raider suddenly came to life, catching the man's wrist from underneath. Pinning him against the bar, the Pinkerton forced the shattered bottle neck back toward the man's own face, dropping it when the razor edge was a few inches from the man's nose.

Then Raider beat the dude against the bar a couple of times, like he was trying to knock dust out of him.

Before he left the saloon, Raider said to the now motionless figure on the floor, "Tell Nick I'm in town."

The man gave no sign he was able to hear. . . .

DEATH'S DEAL

B

BERKLEY BOOKS, NEW YORK

DEATH'S DEAL

A Berkley Book / published by arrangement with
the author

PRINTING HISTORY
Berkley edition/December 1987

ISBN: 0-425-10490-7

A BERKLEY BOOK ® TM 757,375
Berkley Books are published by The Berkley Publishing Group,
200 Madison Avenue, New York, NY 10016
The name "BERKLEY" and the stylized "B" with design
are trademarks belonging to the Berkley Publishing Corporation

PRINTED IN THE UNITED STATES OF AMERICA

10 9 8 7 6 5 4 3 2 1

CHAPTER ONE

The town of Harper had a single street, dusty and wide. In the middle of the day, often nothing disturbed the dust for hours on end. Yet no one in his right mind ever called Harper a sleepy town. When the town wasn't jumping, it lay coiled—like a snake. The place baked in the sun in the parched wilderness of eastern Oregon, at a ferry crossing of the Malheur River. With the melting snows of early summer, the river was now a raging torrent. In a couple of months, it would go back to being a muddy creek.

Two horsemen rode in from the western end of town, their mounts tired and trying to make sideways for the river, where they could smell the water. An old-timer outside the hardware store puffed on his pipe and looked the men over. He opined they were greenhorns, fresh in from back east. One rode clumsily and was clearly not at home in the saddle. The other, decked out in fancy buckskin, with matching tooled leather boots and saddle, rode like he was on military parade. He was obviously a skilled horseman. The trouble was that a poorly broken cow pony did not respond like a thoroughbred to all the fine details of horsemanship as it was taught at the equestrian academies. The old man puffed his pipe and watched. He could tell this much by just looking at the two men, who he could see, now that they were closer, were hardly more than boys. He didn't want to know anything else about them. This was cow country. Out here it was enough to judge a man by the way he rode in the saddle.

The two young men dismounted at the livery stables and led their horses to a water trough. They stretched their limbs.

"I'm beat," the one in the buckskin tunic said. He had a new .45 Peacemaker in a cutaway holster on his right hip. The gun had hand-engraved scrollwork and bone handles, and didn't look as if it had ever been fired.

"You go along," the other said. "I'll put away the horses. Don't forget to tell the landlady there were bedbugs in my mattress last night. I want a different room—or at least a different mattress."

"Way I feel right now, those bedbugs would have to be big as coyotes to keep me awake. I'll tell her." He turned and walked toward the center of town. He had only gone a few paces when a man charged out of the door of the saloon right next to the stables.

"You know a fella by the name of Winthrop Aimesley?" this man growled. He had a few days' growth of beard on his face, and his eyes were bloodshot.

The young man with the shiny gun and expensive

boots stopped. "You're speaking to him. How can I help you?"

"By reaching for your shooting iron."

Aimesley smiled uncertainly. "Are you serious?"

"My name's Bart Noonan. That was my woman you was messing with."

"Oh my God." Aimesley looked wildly around him for a place to hide. There was none. "I assure you, sir, this is a misunderstanding. My intentions were honorable."

"You're dead meat, boy," Bart Noonan growled. "When I'm done with you, they're going to have to bury you to stop your carcass stinking in the street."

"Mr. Noonan, I wish you'd listen—"

"Get out in the street, boy, and reach for your gun like a man. If you don't move, in five seconds flat I'm going to blast you where you stand."

At that moment, behind him Bart heard the snap of a six-gun hammer being cocked. He looked slowly and carefully back over his left shoulder and saw a shabbily dressed young man looking at him over the top of a gun barrel. Bart asked, "Who are you?"

"Jimmy Cluskey. I'm Winthrop's pard, and I reckon while I'm standing here behind your back, he ain't going to come to no harm."

"Only a coward would back-shoot a man," Bart told him.

"You won't be around to accuse me," Cluskey said. "I'll just have to live with my conscience."

Noonan saw that he was in earnest and might in fact shoot him anyway. "Take it easy now, young fella. I think you're going to be on my side when you take a look at this and see what a dirty side-winder your partner is. What he done to me, one day he could do to you." He reached inside his shirt but froze when he saw Cluskey's finger

tighten on the trigger. "I ain't going for no der-
ringer or pocket gun. What I got here is a letter,
written by that snake you call your pard. You take
a look at it and tell me I don't have the right to
call him down in a fair fight. Many's the man who
would have just took the head off his shoulders
with a scattergun, and there ain't a jury west of the
Mississippi that'd find me guilty for it either, not
after they had taken a look at this letter I'm about
to show you." He drew his hand slowly out of his
shirt and held out the folded sheet of paper to
Jimmy Cluskey.

Cluskey kept his battered secondhand Colt trained
on Noonan while he read it.

Darling Odette,
   My heart leaped with excitement at your
smile to me. Yes, yes, I will come to see you. I
hunger for your touch.

Winthrop

Cluskey laughed. "This sounds like the kind of
bullshit Winthrop would write to a woman all right."
   Noonan sneered. "So you admit it's him."
   "There ain't too many dudes with the name of
Winthrop this far west," Cluskey said. "Of course
it's him. But what you don't understand is this.
When Winthrop was talking about her touch, he
meant shaking hands with her. A husband couldn't
leave his wife with a safer man than Winthrop. Even
if she took her clothes off, he wouldn't know what to
do with her."
   This drew hoots of laughter from the onlookers
who had come out of the saloon to see what was
going on and now stood, drinks in hand, waiting to
see blood spilled. Winthrop blushed a deep red at

these comments on his manhood, but he was wise enough to keep his mouth shut.

Bart Noonan saw a way to save face. "I reckon you're right. He don't look like he can shoot, and he don't look like he can fuck. You can put away your gun, Cluskey. I ain't going to pick on that weak-kneed milksap yonder."

Winthrop Aimesley's mouth opened and closed several times, like a fish's, but no sound came out of it. Jimmy Cluskey eased the Colt's hammer onto his thumbnail and from there onto the firing pin, then replaced the weapon in its holster. Bart Noonan spat on the dust, maybe an inch away from one of Winthrop's tooled leather boots, and headed back toward the saloon door.

His way was blocked by a tall skinny man with tangles of dirty yellow hair down to his shoulders, pale blue eyes, and a lantern jaw. Winthrop and Jimmy knew him only as Yaller Dawg, which was how he himself spelled it when he wrote his name. He liked to let people think it was the English version of the name Crow warriors had bestowed on him. He didn't worry about being called yellow, because he was so mean and crazy he wasn't sure what being a coward meant.

Yaller Dawg said to Bart, "That whore you were dumb enough to marry—she was only playing tricks on you, hoping you'd go out and get yourself shot so she could lay her hands on your ranch and your money. She left the letter out where you'd see it, didn't she? When she was a working girl here in town, I had her a dozen times and she never gave me my money's worth. I wouldn't give you a silver dollar for an hour with her on your cleanest sheets."

The men outside the saloon roared with laughter, and Bart Noonan stood still and glared in silent rage. It was one thing for him to call down a sissified Easterner, and quite another to tell this man to go for his gun. Bart was a rancher; Yaller Dawg was a professional gunslinger, a known man-killer.

"You must be talking about some other woman," Bart said finally in a low ,voice made shaky by a tremor of violent anger.

"I ain't. I know the whore you married. I see you with her all the time. Hell, I reckon there ain't a man who was in town back then who don't know her. She was always willing, and she was cheap."

There was nothing for Noonan to do now except creep away on his belly or go for his gun. He went for his gun.

Noonan could have looked like a fast draw up against another cattleman—he would have looked like lightning up against Winthrop Aimesley—but he seemed like he was sleepwalking against a fast-draw artist like Yaller Dawg. Noonan yanked the heavy Colt out of its holster quick enough. It took him a half-second to thumb back the hammer to the cocked position, and another half-second to line up the barrel on the target. He was being too generous when he allowed himself another half-second to squeeze the trigger.

Yaller Dawg meanwhile whipped out his short-barrel Peacemaker. The gun cleared leather fast. The trigger was filed off, and he reached across his body with his left hand and fanned back the hammer spur as far as it would go with the edge of his palm. When he released the hammer, it slammed home on the firing pin. He fanned the hammer back and dropped it a second time.

The first slug caught Bart in the middle of the chest, paralyzing him where he stood. The second bullet hit his body two inches from the entry point of the first. It tunneled into his heart. His cocked revolver dropped from his lifeless fingers and discharged when it hit the ground. The bullet tore up into the sky in front of Yaller Dawg's face.

"Dang bastard nearly got me after all," Yaller Dawg said as he watched Bart Noonan fall. He laughed. "I always reckon that's the way I'm going to die—some tom-fool misfortune crashing down on my head." He slid his smoking gun back into its holster. "Well, you two young fellas don't have nothing to worry about now in the town of Harper."

Jimmy Cluskey shifted his gunbelt on his hips. "We was taking good care of ourselves and didn't need none of your help, mister."

Yaller Dawg laughed like he didn't believe a word of it and went back inside the saloon, followed by the others.

As soon as they were gone, Winthrop turned angrily on Jimmy. "What was all that talk about me not knowing how to handle a woman?"

Cluskey didn't answer him. He just looked at the letter Winthrop had written, which was now lying on the ground at his feet, and then at the unmoving body of Bart Noonan.

John Harrison showed up at the rooming house after dark. He had been gone three days, having left without a word. Aimesley and Cluskey were used to this by now. When the mood hit Harrison, he was best left alone.

"Good to see you, John," Winthrop said in his usual sincere way.

"Yeah, it's a surprise pleasure," Jimmy added sarcastically.

Harrison rounded on him, "Listen, Cluskey, so long as I'm supplying half the cash for this outfit and you're along for a free ride, I'll do what I want and you'll keep your remarks to yourself."

"Now, John, that's not fair," Winthrop put in mildly.

"I don't have to listen to this pauper," Harrison stated bluntly, pointing at Cluskey.

Winthrop was about to protest again but was stopped by Cluskey. "All right, John. I know where I stand with you. You should know where you stand with me. It was my idea for us three to come out here, put a herd together, drive them east to a railhead, and make a fortune. I set everything up. If it weren't for me you two would still be in New York sitting on silk-upholstered chairs, listening to some cousin playing the piano, and maybe having to get up and sing a song and drink tea and be polite in female company. I saved you both from all that."

"Only because you needed us," Harrison pointed out.

"Damn right," Cluskey agreed. "I didn't have a pot to piss in, and you two are rotten with money. I came out here to make some big money fast. You didn't. Neither of you need it. What you came out here for was to prove you can take care of yourselves, prove you're men, show your families you're independent. I don't need to do that. I learnt that long ago on the streets, while you two were learning French and Latin and how to talk to an ambassador. While you was learning to talk with him, I was learning how to pick his pocket. So, John, I know you and me ain't come out here for the same reason."

John Harrison, in his black frock coat and striped pants, looked like the son of a prosperous banker, which he was. He was eighteen years old and had the makings of a mustache on his upper lip. With a long straight nose and protruding chin, he was handsome in a cold, dignified way. He stared at the shabbily dressed Jimmy Cluskey without saying anything. Cluskey was a head shorter than the six-foot-two Harrison. His hair was unruly on his bullet head, which was too big for his body. This gave him a puny look, although in reality he was strongly built in a wiry way. All were the same age, eighteen. Winthrop Aimesley was the least strong of the three. He was a beanpole with fair hair and pale skin—in fact, everything about him seemed pale, weak, washed out. His excessively well-mannered voice and gestures caused men in cattle towns to poke fun at him. They didn't make a joke of Cluskey, who had an air of being quarrelsome and able to take care of himself, nor of Harrison, who was big and hard-looking in spite of his banker's clothes.

"But although us two ain't here for the same reason," Cluskey went on, "we're both here to do the same thing—put a herd together and bring it east to a railroad. Aimesley here does his best. He ain't much use, but he's learning fast. I can't criticize him. But you take off when you feel like it, won't work with us if you don't want to. That ain't no way to put a herd together."

"I always do what I feel like doing," Harrison said with a cold şmile. "So long as you need me for my money to buy those steers, you'll have to put up with me."

Cluskey boiled with fury, but there was nothing he could say to this. Harrison was putting up half the cash for the herd, Aimesley the other half. Once the herd was sold off, they would be repaid their investment and the profit split three ways. Until then Jimmy Cluskey would not earn a nickel. His two partners were footing all the bills for expenses until then. Cluskey needed Harrison more than Harrison needed him. There would come a day, Cluskey told

himself. Until then, patience. And patience was
something that Cluskey did possess. He had learned
it in a hard place, in the East Side slums of New
York.

As the two glowered at each other, Winthrop
Aimesley tried to get their minds onto other things by
saying, "We're taking a run out to a spread first thing
in the morning, John. It would certainly be a pleasure to have you along."

"I'd be glad to go with you, Winthrop," Harrison
said cheerfully.

Cluskey stomped off to his room, leaving the two
rich boys behind to say whatever they liked behind
his back. He was pleased to see that the mattress and
bedding had been changed, but he had lain down for
less than ten minutes when a bedbug bit him. It was
only the first one.

Winthrop Aimesley swung into the saddle next
morning shortly after first light. He grinned at
Cluskey and Harrison, who were saddle-sore after
the previous day's riding and grimaced with dis-
comfort as they bounced on their horses' backs.
His horsemanship was the one thing he could hold
over them, something at which he was clearly a
master and they novices. True, these cayuses were
only half tame and needed firm handling. But he
wasn't afraid of them—and he knew that, deep
down, both Cluskey and Harrison were, having
been thrown, kicked, and even bitten by their
mounts so far.

The hugeness of a horse, with its giant muscular
haunches, its powerful shoulders and neck, the spark
of intelligence in its long skull, could be fairly im-
pressive to any tenderfoot. When the horse also
showed a definite leaning toward wildness and sav-
ageness, and like a lot of animals knew by instinct

who was afraid of it, the tenderfoot had a battle to
fight at the beginning of each day to see who would
be master.

Cluskey lashed out at his animal and yanked on
the steel bit in its mouth. Harrison shouted at his,
dug his spurs in its sides, and cantered his mount
until it tired. He was the one most often thrown.
Although both men changed horses frequently, all
the animals responded to them in much the same
way.

The three rode east for more than two hours before coming to the spread. The rancher and his foreman rode out to meet them.

"My men are putting a bunch into a corral on the
other side of that ridge," the rancher told them.
"They're mostly two-year-olds, like you said you
wanted."

Cow-and-calf combinations and yearlings, because calves were not strong enough for a cattle drive
and yearlings had not flesh enough to be fattened and
slaughtered in the yards. Three-year-olds were ideal,
but these were selling at up to sixteen dollars a head,
which was a lot of money to lay out in the hope of
the animal surviving a long trek in good enough condition to be sold at a profit. They took them when
they could get them for no more than fourteen dollars. Two-year-olds at eight dollars were what they
were looking for, although many ranchers were asking for up to ten dollars a head for these. Generally
they took whatever they were offered if the price was
right.

They rode to a large corral in which about two
hundred beeves were milling around. This corral had
a railed passageway to a smaller one that had a
branding chute. The cowhands had a fire going there,
and Cluskey handed over their branding irons to the
foreman for heating.

"I'll do the branding," Harrison volunteered.

The others nodded their agreement, their roles having gradually become settled by their personalities. Cluskey did the aging of the beeves and the arguing with the rancher. Aimesley kept tally and checked the existing brands.

There were two ways to tell the age: by the horns and by the teeth. There could be no argument with the teeth, but with the horns it was a matter of personal judgment and open to dispute. It was clear to seasoned cattlemen that a young Easterner like Jimmy Cluskey had little experience, so most of them tried to browbeat him and sell him two-year-olds as three-year-olds and so on. They were always a bit surprised at the ferocity of his response, not being used to doing business with New York City slum kids.

A yearling's horns poked an inch or two out of the hide. The horns of a two-year-old had an enlargement or button on the end. The horns were smooth and perfect in a three-year-old, and in a four-year-old the horns showed a ring at the butt. After that, another ring appeared for each year of growth.

"That ain't no four-year-old!" Cluskey shouted angrily, pointing to the beast in question. "There's no ring showing at the base of its horns. You take me for an idiot? Seems like you're as poor a judge of men as you are of cattle."

The rancher looked for a moment as if he was going to belt Cluskey one. Instead he just grunted and said, "Call it a three-year-old, then. I'll give it to you as that for a present."

But this so-called present did nothing to soften up Cluskey. He argued again about the age of another beast.

"What the hell do you know about steers anyhow?" the rancher yelled at him. "I ain't letting no city slicker tell me about beeves. Until a few months ago, the only steer you ever saw was hanging in bits at a butcher's stall."

Cluskey didn't deny this. "I got a sharp eye," he said.

"It takes a man years on the range before he can age steers by the horn. You take my estimates and you won't go far wrong."

"Not by more than a year or two anyway."

The rancher scowled at this, not having much of a sense of humor. But he gave in again, knowing that his only alternative was to count the teeth. If Cluskey proved right, there would be no dealing with him from that point on. What the rancher expected was that he would allow some doubtfuls in Cluskey's favor, and in return would expect some thrown his way. But the New Yorker was all take and no give. Even more infuriating, somehow he had managed to become a damn good judge of a beast's age.

The big problem with aging by teeth was that a wild steer did not show its teeth on request. They had to be looked at by force—by roping the steer, throwing him, and then examining his mouth. The argument between seller and buyer had to grow intense before they went to that much trouble. Sooner or later it always reached that stage when Cluskey was buying. Cluskey nearly always proved right when the teeth were counted, which did not sit well with some men who had been riding herd before Cluskey was born. They cussed out both the steer and Cluskey and said they'd be pleased to be rid of both of them off their land, as if somehow Cluskey and the steer had been in cahoots and pulled a fast one on the rancher.

Winthrop Aimesley sat on the corral's top rail,

tallying each buy in his notebook, with the age and agreed price, along with the animal's brands. He then kept an eye on it until the hands ran it into the next corral, where John Harrison scorched their road mark on the left hip of each beast. Their mark was Circle 9, the numeral inside a circle. The symbol was of no particular significance—Cluskey had bought three branding irons with this on them for a bargain price.

The dust rose in choking clouds as the animals were run around and separated in the corral. Cluskey had learned to be quick on his feet, because some of these half-wild longhorns could be ornery.

When they were all through—the remaining cattle in the large corral being cows and calves, yearlings, and some old steers for which they couldn't agree on a price—Cluskey asked Aimesley how many he had tallied.

"One-twenty," Aimesley shouted.

When the ranch foreman nodded his head in agreement with this, Cluskey said to the rancher, "I'll lay you a deposit of a dollar a head on them in gold and pay you the balance in gold when you drive them out to Eagle Gap this day week."

The rancher agreed and signed his name in Aimesley's tally book.

When Cluskey handed over six twenty-dollar gold pieces, he said, "All we got is your word and signature, but you're the kind of man I have no trouble trusting."

The rancher was in no mood for compliments, since he considered he had received no great price for his cattle. "I have only your word that you'll show up in a week's time to buy. Eagle Gap is nearly fifty miles from here. If you ain't there, a dollar a head is no just compensation for me after all the trouble I've been put to. If you ask me, I'm the one who has to do all the trusting. You know where to find me. Who knows where you fly-by-night Easterners will be in a week's time? Broke, maybe, or in Boot Hill."

Cluskey let him get his dig in and said nothing. He walked through the railed passageway to the smaller corral and branding chute, along with Aimesley, to see how Harrison was doing.

"Take care you brand all the way into the hide," Cluskey told Harrison. "Give them only a hair scorch and it'll grow out in no time."

Harrison said nothing—he only stood there sweating, holding a glowing branding iron, looking after Cluskey as he moved on. He said to Aimesley, "You ever get the feeling of being treated like a hired hand?"

Aimesley shrugged and grinned.

Harrison wasn't smiling.

Jimmy Cluskey and Winthrop Aimesley rode out next morning to another ranch to buy more cattle. John Harrison didn't go along this time, saying he had some business to take care of in town. After a leisurely breakfast, Harrison went to the barber for a shave and then wandered along the boardwalks lining Harper's single wide street, stopping to talk with anyone who was so inclined. When he tired of this, he went into Fletcher's Gold Star Saloon and ordered a beer. In a little while, glass in hand, he wandered back among the tables to watch a poker game, the only one under way this early in the morning. When two of the seven men playing offered to make room for him, he joined the game.

They were playing five-card stud, with no ante and a top bet of five dollars. This was a high enough game for this part of the country, where a ranch hand was well paid if he pulled in sixty or

sixty-five dollars on top of his bed and board. Five
or six hands played and lost could easily take care
of a month's pay. But since there was no ante, a
man could look at his first two cards and drop out
of that hand without it costing him a cent. There
were no chips, only silver dollars and gold pieces,
no greenbacks accepted. No one believed much in
government paper money in eastern Oregon.

Harrison was a cagey player, and he held his
own while he watched and figured out the others.
Two of the men were losing steadily, playing almost every hand and drinking heavily. They were
damned if they were going to be scared off by
money bet into them, and so they lost their cash in
order to show they couldn't be bluffed instead of
sensibly folding when it became probable they'd
been bested. The man who goaded these two mer-
cilessly in bigger and greater errors of judgment
was named Frank Lime.

Lime was no riverboat gambler in fancy clothes.
He had worked as a bank clerk up in Pendleton,
until some sort of misunderstanding had caused him
to leave kind of fast. He had showed up in Harper
with a stake to keep him going for a while. Instead
of finding himself a job, he had made himself a
good living from playing cards most days at the
Gold Star.

John Harrison didn't like him. He had noticed before that anytime some real gamblers happened to be
passing through town, there was no sign of Frank
Lime at the gaming tables. Lime didn't show up
much at night either, when a lot of the rougher sorts
sat down to play.

Lime was having fun. Silver dollars and gold
pieces were heaped in a loose pile on the table in
front of him. He was pleased to change a twenty-
dollar gold piece into silver dollars for Harrison. It

didn't make much difference to the size of his money pile. The two drunks were sore at losing so much. Both being ranch hands, either one of them could have handled the ex-bank clerk easily enough, though he was known to carry a small revolver in his right boot. The problem was that Frank Lime had the backing of the house. It was rumored that he paid ten percent of his winnings to the saloon owners for protection. Like most saloons, the Gold Star always had someone on hand to take care of trouble. Although drunk, both the cowboys knew that an argument or fight at the bar could happen to a bishop, but messing up a card game was serious business. If they didn't like what was happening to them here, they could always go somewhere else. They intended doing that—right after they had won back some of their losses.

Harrison didn't spot what was going on until he lost two big pots in a row to Lime. The cards were marked. The intricate floral pattern on their backs varied slightly for jacks, queens, kings, and aces. It was only an extra leaf on a corner branch for jacks, six instead of five flower petals for queens —very hard to notice in the intricate pattern unless a man knew where to look—and yet Frank Lime could tell at a glance whether another player's hole card, face down on the table, was any one of these.

Instead of exposing him, John Harrison had a better idea. He would use Lime's scheme against him.

The next hand, he was dealt a Jack as his hole card and a three face up. Lime's ace being the highest exposed card, he led off the betting by throwing a silver dollar in the pot. Three players dropped out, and the dealer dealt another card face up to each of the five players still in the game. Harrison connected with a pair of threes, so the betting went to him. John carefully let his eyes wander to each man's hole card. Lime had a king face down, the others nothing, so far as he could tell from the marked cards. Another dollar each went in the pot and five more cards were dealt face up. Harrison's pair of threes was still the best hand, so he set the betting again with another dollar in the pot from each man who wanted to go on playing. All five stayed in the game.

The fifth card was dealt face up, and the player on Frank Lime's left made a pair of sixes. This man checked, not wanting to bet into the table, and Harrison went along with that, knowing that if his pair of threes bet into a pair of sixes, his bet would be seen. The play came around to Lime, who threw a five-dollar gold piece into the pot. The pair of sixes folded, as did the next two players. Lime looked expectantly at the last player left. His face was expressionless, his gaze unblinking.

John Harrison knew that Frank Lime's ace and ten showing were not backed up by his hole card, which was a king. He saw Lime's five and raised him another five.

Fast as a blink, Lime raised him again. Harrison came back at him. Lime flipped his cards face down and pushed them toward the deck. Harrison scraped in the pot.

Lime had a thoughtful look on his face. He knew that Harrison had beaten him with a pair of threes, his hole card having been a jack. He was not a man to sit around while suspicion lingered. Getting to his feet fast, he gathered up the cards before the next dealer could reach them. He said, "Fellas, I have to go."

"All right, Frank," one of the players said. "But leave the cards. We ain't quitting."

"These are beat up," Lime said. "Get another deck from the house."

"Hell, no," Harrison put in. "That's my lucky deck. I'm staying with those cards. Give them here to me." He was on his feet too.

Harrison had no intention of exposing Lime's cheating, wanting only to put the cards to his own profit and hang on to them for use elsewhere. Frank Lime saw only the threat of exposure. He had taken a bagful of coins off these men, and they were not the sort to take kindly to news of cheating. Having seen a man tarred and feathered once in Pendleton, there was no way he was going to let that or worse happen to him. He stuffed the deck of cards in his coat pocket.

Harrison went for his gun. He had been practicing his draw for an hour each day and he was getting fast. He leveled the barrel of his Starr Army .44 on Lime's gut and squeezed the trigger of the double-action revolver. The hammer rose and fell as the chambers turned. The round-nosed .44 slug was propelled out of the barrel by the powder blast in the brass cartridge, and it tore through the gambler's abdominal muscles, which were not much developed anyway.

Lime gasped as he felt the hot lump of lead tear through his insides. His right hand jerked out of his pocket. All it was holding was the deck of cards. He collapsed groaning on the sawdust floor of the saloon.

"I thought he was pulling a gun," John Harrison said lamely.

"Bullshit," one onlooker said. "How could he draw a gun with a deck of cards in his hand?"

Harrison argued, but no one was threatening to lynch him anyway, because no one was all that fired up anyway about the death of a gambler who had been fleecing everyone in town. When the marshal came, he said some unkind things about newly arrived Easterners and demanded that Harrison pay for the burial of Lime, who was by now almost dead, except for real shallow breathing and an occasional twitch.

Before he left the saloon, John Harrison reached down and gathered up the deck of marked cards.

CHAPTER TWO

The two portly gentlemen removed their top hats as they were shown into the office of Allan Pinkerton, at the headquarters of the Pinkerton National Detective Agency on Chicago's Fifth Avenue. They settled their bulk comfortably into leather chairs before the big mahogany desk and were told that Mr. Pinkerton would be with them presently. Having lit up large cigars, they contemplated the ceiling while they waited. They had come to Chicago from New York City by train and somewhere in Pennsylvania had run out of business topics to discuss. Neither was much given to small talk.

Allan Pinkerton entered his office, a bearded, domineering bear of a man, whose large size consisted of muscle and bone, unlike the lard of the two fat cats seated before his desk. Brief introductions over, they got down to business.

"Mr. Pinkerton, I need hardly tell you that a bank

the size of the one of which I am president has investigative agents at our beck and call," the one named Harrison said.

Pinkerton nodded to show he thought this probable.

Harrison went on, "Mr. Aimesley here also has access to skilled investigators in the business world. Through our mutual efforts, we have located our missing sons, but have been unable to persuade them to return. Let me explain. His boy and mine are in eastern Oregon. We tracked them through their dealings with local banks. When our agents arrived on the scene to bring them home, they found themselves in unfamiliar circumstances. These men are knowledgeable and capable, able to find their way around any big city, experienced in the ways of the world. But they are not trained to function in the wilderness. In short, Mr. Pinkerton, our agents were able to *locate* our sons, but could not *enforce* their return."

"Any violent incident?" Pinkerton inquired mildly in his Scottish burr.

"Not quite," Harrison replied. "However, my son is reported to have fired a pistol at the feet of one agent, forcing him to lift his feet in dance movements in order to avoid being hit."

"A charming western custom," Pinkerton said with a smile. "I can see that your boys are becoming acclimated out there. Something you said earlier interested me. You mentioned that you had traced your sons through their dealings with Oregon banks. They have funds?"

"Ample, I'm afraid," Harrison said. "My son John's money was being held in trust for him until he reached the age of twenty-one. By a simple maneuver, which our family lawyer overlooked, John was able to get his hands on a large quantity of his railroad and cotton stocks. He simply sold them on the exchange and banked the proceeds."

"My son Winthrop," Aimesley said, "has always been such a good boy and dutiful son, it never occurred to me that precautions might be needed when he inherited the entire fortune of his great-aunt, who adored him as a child."

Pinkerton looked at them both and said patiently, "Hasn't it occurred to you that these two healthy young men are just sowing some wild oats and that when they tire of this they will return to the fold?"

Harrison snapped, "I have heard that both of your sons work hard in this office under your supervision, Mr. Pinkerton, and that you are the last man in the world who would tolerate either of them sowing wild oats."

"I am inclined to be strict," Pinkerton conceded.

"Then you and I are in agreement. I should also add that the son of a business associate of mine was recently shot dead during a bank raid in Missouri. I naturally assumed he had been working in the bank and was shocked to learn he had been one of the raiders. Think of it—his father a prominent banker and his son a dead bank robber. The family was fortunate that the gutter press did not get hold of it."

"I think we should mention," Aimesley put in, "that our sons have come under the malevolent influence of a person their own age. His name is Jimmy Cluskey. He seems to have lived in the streets in one of our more disreputable New York residential neighborhoods. His freedom and ragamuffin ways made him something of a hero to boys reared in the confines of straitlaced families. I think I can understand that. This Cluskey no doubt was a charming street urchin but, like most of them, became a dangerous criminal in his late teens. Apparently no longer content to prey on the purses of elderly inebriated gentlemen late at night, he has seized control of the minds of our sons, taken them beyond our reaches to the frontier wilderness, and engaged them as financiers and assistants in his evil schemes."

"Which are?" Pinkerton asked.

"I don't know what they are doing," Aimesley said.

"They claimed to be cattlemen," Harrison added, "but neither of those boys knows anything about livestock, and I doubt that Cluskey could tell a cow from a sheep."

"So what you want from me," Allan Pinkerton said, "is someone to confront Cluskey and bring your underage sons home, probably against their will. The two young men have lots of money and are in lawless territory. I have one of my best operatives finishing up a case not far from where your sons are. His name is Raider, and I can assure you that his personality fits in well with conditions in eastern Oregon. I'll send him some assistants. I suppose that expenses will not be an important consideration?"

"Spend what you like," Harrison said, and Aimesley readily nodded his consent.

Pinkerton smiled. These were the sort of clients he liked. "What about Cluskey?" he asked. "Do we bring him back too?"

Harrison answered, "Mr. Pinkerton, I have too much respect for you and your agency to ask that you do anything illegal. It would be ideal, though, if your people could find some way of keeping Cluskey permanently on the far side of the Mississippi."

The pony shied and threw its rider. The thirteen-year-old boy picked himself up out of the dust and cursed at his horse, which stood a little distance away, snorting and bug-eyed with fear, tossing its head. Then the boy saw what had spooked his mount

—a rattler, a big one, almost five feet long. He made his way to the pony, keeping an eye on the place where the reptile lay coiled, its head slowly moving from side to side about a foot off the ground. Pulling his repeater from its saddle sling, he levered a shell into the chamber and raised the rifle to his shoulder. He found the foresight bead in the rearsight notch and centered it on the rattlesnake's head. He squeezed the trigger and saw the venomous snake's head blow apart into fragments.

His pony was jumpy and nervous all the way back to the ranch house because it sensed that the snake was in the burlap bag tied to the saddle horn. The animal would have bolted if the boy had not held it on a tight rein. When he emptied the bag's contents onto the kitchen table in the ranch house kitchen, his mother screamed. She never failed to do that when he brought a snake home. It was an instinct with her, he figured, like the pony. She wouldn't even touch it until after he had skinned it and chopped it in sections. Then she was pleased enough to have it. Times had been hard since his father had died two years past. Meat was scarce on their table.

While his mother prepared dinner, the boy went out in the yard to help his younger brother finish the farm chores. They had fifty cattle and two hundred head of sheep and grew corn in fields down by the river. Their uncle—their mother's brother—had a spread a ways down the valley, and he came by frequently to lend a hand and give advice or encouragement.

"Get me my gun," the older boy ordered the younger in a tone of voice that meant he was not kidding.

The younger boy looked across the level land toward the river and saw a rider approaching. The sun was beginning to set behind him and made it hard to see who it was. "That ain't Uncle Jake," the younger boy judged and ran to obey his brother's order. He came running back with the Winchester repeater and a fistful of spare shells. "Plug the bastard if he don't draw up nicely and state his business."

"Take it easy," the older boy said, proud of his maturity. "Don't go forgetting the time we nearly killed the sheriff's deputy."

"Son of a bitch ain't been back since, has he, collecting county taxes? But this don't look like no deputy or law-abiding person to me. I say we give him a warning shot, down close near the top of his hat."

The older boy decided this wasn't such a bad suggestion. He didn't much like the looks of this stranger either. Besides, the shot would serve to warn their mother, who would look out the window and see the stranger riding in. They could see him clearly now. He wore a black Stetson and a black leather jacket. His face was tanned, and a black mustache curved out from his nostrils and turned sharply inward at the corners of his mouth. The boy raised his rifle to fire a warning shot.

Suddenly a big revolver was in the approaching rider's hand. He was still more than a hundred yards off and the advantage lay with the rifle, since even an expert could miss with a revolver at that range. But this was not what was going through the boy's head. He saw the calm, deadly way the six-gun was waiting on him to make a move with his rifle, and he knew for sure, just from the easy air of certainty the stranger had, that he was already outmatched, even at this distance. He lowered the repeater's barrel so it pointed to the ground a few yards in front of him, and the rider responded by putting his shooting iron back in its holster.

"Your pa around?" he called to the boys.

"Maybe."

"Go tell him the Clark bunch has been seen riding toward this part of the valley."

"They never come out this way, mister. There ain't nobody worth robbing that lives hereabouts."

"They're on the run."

"Who's chasing them?" the younger boy asked.

"Me," the stranger said.

The boys were impressed. One man alone chasing Mad Harry Clark and his collection of varmints! Everyone the boys knew were scared shitless of Mad Harry and never even bothered to pretend otherwise, although for the most part Harry let the farming folk be.

"Go tell your pa I want to buy my supper and put up for the night in that barn," the stranger told them.

"He ain't around."

"Then tell your mother." The big man reached behind him into a saddlebag, hauled out a side of bacon, and tossed it down to the older boy, who dropped his rifle in order to catch it. The man smiled at the boy's mistake in letting go his weapon for precious food, and he kept a wary eye on the younger brother after he picked up the Winchester.

"What if she says no?" the one holding the bacon asked.

"Tell her to send the food out if she ain't comfortable about me being in the house. And tell her that with me sleeping the night in the barn, she don't have to worry about the Clark bunch coming here in the middle of the night."

They watched him dismount and looked up at him as he towered over them. He was maybe a head taller than their father had been, and his shoulders were so wide that to come in their ranch house door, as well as having to duck, he might have to turn sideways. They had never seen anyone as big as this, and they stood there staring at him with their mouths open

until he shooed them away and said he was going to
water his horse.

Their mother, frightened at the presence of an unseen stranger out in the barn, plied her sons with
questions, glanced out the windows every time she
passed them, and jumped at the least unexpected
sound. After a while her curiosity began to get the
better of her fear. From her sons' description, the
stranger certainly sounded interesting. Hers was a
lonely life in the valley. She drove the wagon eight
miles to church every Sunday morning and lingered
after the services to talk with her neighbors. Her
brother came by all the time, but he was more given
to work than conversation. Now here she was with
this downright interesting stranger out in her barn
and she without adult company from one week to
another.

"The food is ready," she told her boys. "Holler for
him to come in."

Her sons gave her a shocked look. The eldest
said, "The fella said it was all right to bring his chow
out to him."

The younger added, "None of us would be safe
with him in here."

To their astonishment, she smiled. "If he's going
to try something, he'll be just as likely to try from
out there as in here. Maybe if we ask him in and
show him that we're nice folk, he'll take too much of
a liking to us to want to harm us."

The boys looked unconvinced but knew when
their mother was decided and it was hopeless to
argue. They moved toward the door.

She called after them, "Better not say it's rattlesnake we're eating for dinner. Some folk are per-
nickety about things like that."

After the boys brought him in, they watched him

as he talked with their mother. They could see right off that he was just like them—he had no idea what to say to women. However, this was no problem with their mother, because she liked to talk on and on, the only thing needed being someone to listen. His name was Raider, and he was a Pinkerton who was hunting down Mad Harry Clark for a killing they had heard about.

All Raider said was, "This time Clark killed the wrong man, and he's going to pay for it. The man he gunned down ran the Yankee Belle mine down in the Jackson Mountains for an eastern mining concern. He was traveling with the mine's payroll and expenses for a month. Mad Harry's got six Pinkertons combing these parts for him, with orders to take him dead or alive. I'm one of those six, and I aim to be the one to nail him."

The boys soon got over their awe and, in spite of their mother's warning, brought up the subject of snakes. They told Raider about some of the big rattlers they had seen in the valley. He agreed with them that horses had a special dread of snakes and told them about some of the close calls he had had. Then he complimented their mother on her cooking as he helped himself to a large mouthful.

"That ain't nothing but plain farmyard chicken," she said.

"It tastes mighty good to a man who don't often get to eat home cooking, ma'am," Raider told her.

The younger boy piped up, "I hear rattlesnake makes real good eating."

Raider dropped his fork and stared at the boy with blazing eyes. He grated, "If anyone fed me snake meat, I'd shoot them dead on the spot."

He slowly picked up his fork and began to eat again, while the two boys watched him in terrified silence.

Their mother asked, "More chicken, Mr. Raider?"

"I don't mind if I do, ma'am."

The boys were proud of her. That took some nerve.

Raider hadn't fully dropped off to sleep when he heard footsteps outside the barn. Whoever was moving out there was doing so without a light in the total darkness. His hand fumbled for his revolver and pulled it beneath the blankets so he could pull back the hammer without the metallic click being heard. Gun cocked, he eased away from the mattress on the floor and stood in his longjohns against one wall, waiting for the door to open.

The heavy timber door creaked softly on its rusty hinges as it was slowly and carefully opened. Someone entered and closed the door after them. The person made for where the mattress lay and poked about there.

"Mr. Raider?" It was a female voice.

"I was just standing over here ready to shoot, ma'am. Sneaking up on me like that ain't the safest thing in the world to do."

"I was just bringing you an extra blanket," she said. "I thought you might be cold."

"That's right kind of you, ma'am," he said, laying down the gun to find the candle and matches.

The candle flame wavered in the drafty barn. By its light, she spread the blanket over those already on the mattress. Raider climbed in beneath them and beckoned to her. She lost no time in wriggling out of her long dress and petticoats. She stood in her underclothes and asked, "You going to take off them longjohns?"

"Yes, ma'am," Raider responded and went about removing the red flannel garment.

She removed her lacy undergarments and slipped

under the blankets next to him. She said, "That's the second time you nearly shot me in just a few hours. First time was over the food."

Raider laughed. "I took a rise out of your kids with that."

"So you knew!"

"Down in Texas we used to call rattler's meat desert chicken, so you weren't too far wrong in what you called it."

He allowed his hand to glide slowly down her soft, smooth skin in a gentle caress. She was shy and nervous at first, having grown unaccustomed to a man's touch. He relaxed her with his easy, unhurried stroking hands, and she let him draw her close to him in a hot, tight embrace.

His hard cock pressed against her belly. She freed one arm and her hand traveled down. Her fingers touched his distended member, and she softly felt it from the thick patch of pubic hair out to its bulbous end. While she was doing this, Raider placed his hands on both her breasts and gently but firmly squeezed, releasing them only to tease her nipples with his fingertips.

He felt her urgently pushing her body beneath him, parting her legs and pulling him toward her. He felt the head of his cock slide into her warm, moist sex, and he drove his mighty shaft firmly into her yielding depths.

Rather than striking out across country, Clark and his gang had stayed in the valley of the Quinn River, west of the Santa Rosa range in northern Nevada. Raider had bet on their doing this. They were just a catch-all bunch who came together and went their own ways as opportunity offered. They weren't tightly organized and probably had made no provision for a hideout in inaccessible country. It wasn't all that easy to disappear into the mountains or the deserts without ending up as food for the grizzlies or coyotes. From what Raider could tell, this crowd had been having it soft. They had got used to moving only far enough to tire out whoever was chasing them, and not a mile farther. But the Pinkertons had thrown them for a loop by just not quitting.

In his usual way, Raider had struck out on his own, and for the past couple of days he had lost contact with the other Pinkerton operatives. During these two days he had followed Mad Harry and five of his men along the east bank of the river, though without catching sight of them. He inquired in homesteads along the way. The outlaws had stopped to buy food or sleep in a bunkhouse or barn overnight in some of them. They had robbed nobody, careful not to turn the locals against them at this time. They knew they were being hunted, possibly by all six Pinkertons. Sooner or later they would loop back and find out how many, if any, were still on their trail.

To protect himself against that time, Raider was putting out word to everyone he met that the Pinkertons were interested only in Mad Harry, not the members of his gang. They too had probably been involved in the killing of the mine manager, but only Harry Clark had been identified for certain. Raider hoped that some if not all of the gang would desert Harry when they heard that the heat was off them. These were dangerous times to be a pard of Harry Clark's.

After he finished a breakfast of bacon, biscuits, and strong coffee, Raider rode out from the ranch house. The sun was only just above the Santa Rosas, and there was still a chill in the air. He needed to learn where Mad Harry had spent the night and decide on his next move there. No one had seen any of the Clark bunch in the farms farther along the valley.

He might suspect some of keeping their mouth shut but not everybody. And nothing moved in the valley that wasn't noticed by these farmers. Even if Clark had tried to push through in the dead of night, their dogs would have raised the alarm. There was only one conclusion Raider could come to—somehow he had overshot Clark and his men. Right now they might even be doubling back, retracing their steps and leaving him to chase empty air away up the river.

He rode back, not stopping at any of the houses, just keeping a wary eye out for riders. The few men he came across had seen nobody that day, apart from Raider himself. The farmers kept mostly to their own holdings, and no one did much traveling in these parts except to go to town for supplies or church on Sunday. Some of the farmers made it clear to Raider that he was no more welcome in the valley than Mad Harry.

When he saw the dust raised by a galloping horse up ahead, he pulled his carbine from the saddle scabbard and tried to recognize the figure in the saddle as Clark. He couldn't, because the horse was being ridden bareback and the rider was a kid—the younger one at the farm where he had spent the night. He was some horseman! The kid's legs weren't long enough to grip the sides of the big colt, so he was almost astride the neck of the animal as it ran, somehow hanging on and staying up there.

"I been looking for you!" he yelled to Raider, after he reined the horse in so hard it reared on its hind legs, fit to make a cavalry officer proud. "Mad Harry and his men came to our place and my brother fired on them with his repeater. He didn't hit no one, and they took off because I reckon they didn't want to stay around with the noise from all my brother's shooting. But as they were going, Mad Harry shouted that he'd show ignorant farmers like us to be more friendly. He said he was going to come back and cut our throats. I reckon he knows my pa is dead. Anyway they went on a piece, and when I sneaked out on this here horse, they had stopped to eat—I guess—at a place near us. My brother is guarding our mother. He says to get your ass back there quick as you can."

Raider was already moving. "Let's go."

They moved fast along the trail. The boy pointed to his left, away from the river, and Raider followed him away from the trail behind some low scrub-covered hills. They stopped near the top of one of the hills, and Raider looked down on a small farmhouse with five horses tied to a corral rail in front of it.

"There were six when I passed here last," the kid said. "Mad Harry is gone back to cut their throats!"

After that, Raider found it hard to keep up with him. He was light and had a young, rested horse. Raider was heavy, and his mount had been ridden hard for several days, plus the fact it was not a very good horse in the first place. He caught up with the kid when the latter slowed as they neared the farm. Down toward the river, they saw a saddled horse tied in the shade of some willows.

"That's Mad Harry's," the kid declared. "You see how he tied it out of sight from the house. Right now he's sneaking up on them. Or maybe he's already inside, carving them with his knife."

Raider had to grab at the bridle of the boy's horse to restrain him. "You've done your bit. From now on leave things to me. Show me the back way to your barn. My guess is that Clark would try to sneak into the barn unobserved, and from there make a charge on the house when the moment was right. Since we don't see him nowhere moving toward the house, there's a chance he's watching from the barn at this moment. We need to move in quiet."

This they did. They drew the horses up and left them on grass while they walked the last couple of hundred yards to the structure. Raider tried to make the kid stay behind, saying that he had spent the night there, he needed no help in finding his way around the barn. But the kid wasn't having any of it, so Raider gave him his carbine and told him to walk along as his backup.

They climbed a ladder to the hayloft and, moving silently across the soft hay, looked down through spaces between boards into the barn beneath. A man was crouched in the open doorway of the barn, cradling a rifle and staring intently at the house. One of the barn doors and the dimness inside shielded him from view from the house.

The kid was already raising Raider's carbine to his shoulder for a shot between the floorboards of the hayloft. Raider pushed the barrel aside and pointed to himself. The kid reluctantly nodded.

Raider still didn't trust him, so he whispered, "There's a reward of five hundred dollars for Mad Harry. I'll take him alive and make sure you and your family collect it."

The boy nodded his agreement more convincingly this time.

Raider moved forward over the hay until he came to an open space. He peered down. Clark was not directly beneath the opening. Raider would not be able to leap directly on him. It was maybe a ten-foot drop to the board floor beneath—and Raider didn't want to wait around for something to go wrong. Placing his left hand on the edge, he leaped over and landed on his feet on the floor beneath with a thunderous crash.

It took the big Pinkerton several moments to regain his balance, but it took Mad Harry Clark even longer to get over his fright. Raider had landed about ten feet away from him, making the floorboards tremble and vibrate like a major earthquake had hit. Now he bounded across at Clark before the outlaw could bring his rifle barrel to bear on him. He caught him in a flying tackle as Clark stood upright and tried to move out of his way. Both men crashed to the floor.

Raider felt for his opponent's face with his right hand while he drove his left elbow hard into his solar plexus. He twisted his thumb into Clark's left eye socket, and the outlaw had to squeeze his eyes tightly shut to prevent his eyeball from being gouged out. Clark's hat having fallen off, the Pinkerton grabbed a fistful of hair and used it to hammer the back of Mad Harry's head on the floor until he grew peaceful. Then he dragged him by one boot out into the sunshine.

The older brother came out of the ranch house door, rifle in hand, a look of amazement on his face. "I never saw either of you," he admitted.

"You sure this is Mad Harry?" Raider asked, pointing to the unconscious man. When the boy nodded, Raider said, "I thought so, but I been wrong before. Them pictures on wanted posters sometimes ain't too lifelike, if you ask me. You'll find my horse back of the barn along with your colt." He turned to the younger brother, who had emerged from the barn. "Don't forget to give me my carbine back, but hang on to it while you collect this cuss's horse from over in those willows. If Clark's sidekicks show, you just begin shooting and I'll be right along."

When the boys were gone, their mother brought Raider a cup of coffee. She said, "Pity you don't have time to stay around for something else."

Raider smiled. But their friendly talk was soon cut

short when Harry Clark opened his eyes and his mouth.

He told the woman, "I'm gonna take my Bowie and twist its blade you know where."

This earned him a boot from Raider on the side of his head. Not even this shut him up.

"You ain't never gonna take me out of this valley," he shouted. "My boys is gonna blast you soon as you try to ride out of here. How do you think you're gonna get through them hills downriver from here? They'll drill you for sure, you big lug."

Raider thanked him for this information. Then, after the horses were brought, he made Clark sit on the chestnut that he himself had used to follow the outlaws, tying his wrists to the saddle with a rawhide thong. He tied the man's ankles to each other with a longer thong beneath the belly of the horse, so he couldn't dismount. Picking up Mad Harry's hat, which was light brown with an eagle feather sticking up on one side, Raider put it on and placed his own black Stetson on Clark's head.

"What about the reward?" the younger brother demanded.

"What reward?" the older one wanted to know.

"I didn't want to say anything about it last night," Raider explained, "in case you two young men got some wild notions about how to make a fast dollar. There's a reward for five hundred on this fella, dead or alive. Seems to me all three of you have earned it well."

"We'll share it with you," the older boy offered, in spite of getting a dirty look from the younger.

"Us Pinkertons ain't allowed to accept. I'll see to it that it comes your way." He waved to them, and, after making a present to them of the outlaw's rifle and six-gun, he moved out with his prisoner.

* * *

"I can see what you mean about these hills," Raider observed conversationally to Harry Clark.

Mad Harry was looking crazy by now, jerking this way and that, his eyes rolling in his head. He was wearing Raider's hat and riding Raider's chestnut horse. From a distance, his black shirt looked much like the Pinkerton's black leather jacket. Meanwhile Raider was on Clark's gray horse and wearing his brown hat with a feather. Harry could see a lot of potential for a bad mistake. These were the hills he had sworn the Pinkerton would never ride through alive. On the way, they had passed farmers who had all gawked to see him trussed up like a chicken being taken to market. Some of them had taken off at a run to spread the news. It couldn't have been long before his men had heard. They would come after him to free him. Harry only hoped their eyesight was good and that maybe they were using their brains today. He looked up at the hills all around them and saw scores of places a rifleman could hide to bushwhack them. It was driving him crazy.

Raider meanwhile was smiling and talkative. As always, circumstances that made most other men shiver and sweat with fright only made him relaxed and easy. What made Raider sweat was to have to sit in an overfurnished parlor, with a cup and saucer in his hands, trying to think of something polite to say. Bloodthirsty lowlifes like Harry Clark he knew how to handle with no problem.

But Raider was keeping the hat brim low over his face and was also keeping a sharp lookout for anyone near enough at hand to tell the difference between them. Some of those farmers may have seen—yet Raider guessed they were so pleased by what they thought they saw, they didn't examine it any closer.

A man is more easily persuaded when the news is good.

Mad Harry made a kind of grunting noise a couple of seconds before Raider heard the shot. He stiffened in the saddle, then stood nearly upright in the stirrups, his wrists bound to the saddle holding him down. His eyes were wide and staring straight ahead. He extended his head and neck forward as if he were trying to see something through a fog. Blood spurted from his open mouth, onto the horse's mane.

The animal was stamping nervously, but Mad Harry was holding him by a tight rein. Every time Harry breathed out after gasping in some air, another spurt of blood issued from his mouth onto the horse's neck. The chestnut was getting spooked from the smell of blood and the peculiar behavior of the rider.

The Pinkerton heard the slap of the next bullet as it plowed through Clark's rib cage. He was already falling sideways out of the saddle when the sound of the shot came and then reverberated through the hills. His bound wrists and ankles prevented him from falling to the ground. Since he hung on the far side of the horse from the gunman, it would have looked like he had been blown out of the saddle.

Raider soothed the horse with words as best he could, but it was probably only the animal's weariness that stopped it from bolting. The Pinkerton held up his two hands above his head, as if they were bound. He did his best to make a beckoning gesture while still keeping the hat brim low over his face.

Five riders emerged from behind the shoulder of a hill about four hundred yards away. They were waving their hats and whooping in true cowboy style. Come another hundred yards, and he'd give them something to holler about.

The men came on, delighted to have freed their leader. Raider scooped the carbine out of its saddle scabbard, worked the lever, and threw off a fast shot, levered in a second shell, shot again. He knocked two men out of the saddle with those first two shots. Only then did the remaining three realize they had been suckered into a trap.

Raider nailed a third one in the back of the neck as he tried to ride away. The other two put part of a hillside between them and him. He knew the kind they were. They wouldn't cause any more trouble. In fact they wouldn't quit riding till they had crossed the county line, or near enough, since Humboldt County was too big to ride across in a day.

He tied Harry Clark's body over the back of the outlaw's own gray and took his chestnut down to the riverbank to wash off the blood on its mane and neck. Then he mounted his horse and set off downriver, leading the gray behind.

The bodies of the three outlaws lay where they had fallen, and their horses grazed on a hillside. Raider would not mention these men in his report to Chicago. There was no way he was going to do all the paperwork needed.

CHAPTER THREE

At last the cattle drive was under way. Jimmy Cluskey, Winthrop Aimesley, and John Harrison had gathered more than eight hundred head and began the push east. They aimed to snowball eight hundred to three thousand by buying additional cattle as they traveled. For a while, with all their troubles and misunderstandings, it looked like the whole thing might fall through. But Cluskey hadn't let that happen. Unlike the other two, he had nothing to fall back on. This was Cluskey's big break. This was it for him. If he had to drive those longhorns east to the railroad on his hands and knees, he would do it.

They had hired some hands to ride with the herd and set about gathering the bunches they had purchased into one big crowd. Some of the longhorns didn't take kindly to each other, and some of the men hired didn't know what they were doing. Two men quit, and a few of the cattle ran off in the middle of

41

the night—Cluskey wasn't sure if these events were connected. The long days riding herd wore down even Harrison, and he was pleasanter than usual, glad to wolf down his chow and crawl wearily under his blankets near the camp fire.

Once they got the animals moving over open rangeland, things settled down. Cluskey had been doing some talking with drovers, and a few of their hired hands had been on cattle drives before—or said they had. The idea was to get the herd moving in the shape of a wedge. Cluskey had been told that a certain number of animals—up to two hundred in a herd of three thousand—become the leaders. Of these, the same six or seven steers are always out front, at the point of the wedge. All the men soon got to know these steers by sight.

When the herd was moving, a rider took position on either flank to point the leaders. It took four or five men to drive on the cattle at the rear of the herd, known as the drag, and this was called pounding them on the back, although it involved cussing and horsework more than that. Already cripples and worn-out critters were dropping back, and they couldn't be allowed to slow the herd. From one bunch of fat cattle they bought, two keeled over and died when being driven uphill.

"It was their hearts," Harrison said. "My Uncle Herbert went down like that one afternoon on the carpet in the dining room. Dead as a doornail. We'd just finished Sunday dinner, and I remember noticing he hadn't been able to pull his chair close to the table because of his huge belly. I looked down at him on the floor and he had the same look in his eyes that these two steers have, a kind of hopeless gaze."

"So if you see any more steers that remind you of your Uncle Herbert," Cluskey said, "remind us not to buy them. Come on. Let's keep moving, men. Cook, you take one man and butcher them steers. No reason why we should leave prime steak for the buzzards."

They hoped to make an average of seven or eight miles a day. However, the distance they made in a day depended on things they couldn't control, like the availability of water or grazing, the weather, whether they had hills or rivers to cross, the contrariness of the steers. One day they made thirteen miles over flat ground. Another day they made five, after riding herd for more than fifteen hours. They soon learned the benefit of sending a man ahead each day to scout for the easiest routes and for grass and water.

At sundown they looked for a bed ground for the steers, a level place on high ground, free of sagebrush, and not too far from water. When darkness fell the steers lay down, and two men circled the herd slowly on horseback from opposite directions. They kept about fifty yards out from the nearest animals and sang lullabies when the animals showed signs of restlessness, mostly caused by one steer horning another in order to steal its warm bed. Round about midnight the animals got up, as they always did, stretched themselves, and lay down on their other side.

The others enjoyed an exhausted sleep in their blankets around the embers of the fire. The last thing each man had done before turning in was to see that his bridle, saddle, and rope were close to him and ready to throw on a horse. A night stampede was the worst—the most dangerous to the men and with the most potential for permanent loss of beasts. Like firemen, they listened with one ear for the alarm while they slept.

The camp cook crept out from beneath his blankets at three in the morning. He was a drunken, disagreeable fellow who had a mind of his own, but he cooked good chow, and that was what mattered.

Also, he was considerate enough to go about his early morning work quietly, so as not to wake the sleeping men before their time.

Cluskey, lying on the ground in a deep sleep, suddenly awoke as something moved in the darkness before his face. It rattled loudly inches from his nose, and his heart beat wildly even after he realized it was a spur on a moving boot. The bastard was whistling in that annoyingly cheerful way that folk often have who like to get up before anyone else. He had probably heard the cook moving about, and so he had put on his spurs and chaps, rolled up his blankets, and stomped around among the sleeping bodies, nearly driving his heel into Cluskey's mouth and his spur into his eye. Cluskey hoped one of the others would shoot him.

The men rose shortly before first light and ate steak and biscuits washed down by strong coffee. There was all the food any man could eat, and they stuck their knives into large fried steaks, knowing it might be sundown or even later before they got a chance to eat again, if the day proved rough. John Harrison didn't seem interested in food. He wandered off to the top of a nearby bluff and stood there by himself, staring out across the country that the sun was beginning to light up, smoking cigarette after cigarette. The cook called to him repeatedly, but Harrison ignored him.

While they were finishing the meal, the wrangler got the horses together. They were taking well to the bell mare and causing no trouble. The docile old mare had a cowbell tied around her neck. Out of habit, the other horses stayed within earshot of the bell during the hours of darkness, unless something alarmed them or they were thirsty and smelled water. Unlike cattle, horses could not be herded close together overnight because they didn't rest properly at

close quarters to one another. To be a good wrangler,
a man had to have a special feeling for horses and
understand their needs.

The wrangler tied a rope about fifty feet long to
the top of one of the chuck wagon's front wheels,
and a similar length to the top of one rear wheel.
Two men picked up the loose ends and walked away
from the chuck wagon until they had pulled the ropes
taut, forming a corral. The others drove the horses
into it. Any of the horses could easily have broken
through the ropes or jumped them, but they didn't,
not liking them and keeping their distance.

The men walked in among almost forty horses, all
broncos recently broken, and they pushed and shoved
as they selected their mounts for the day. Cluskey
and Harrison were still a bit nervous about this, expecting to be kicked or trampled—but even the wild-
est among the horses always avoided contact with the
men in their midst. Each man had six horses assigned
to him, and Cluskey intended to buy more as they
hired more hands to tend the growing herd. Everything depended on their horses, and they had been
warned not to stint on fresh mounts.

Harrison came back while the men were saddling
their horses and the cook was cleaning up. He demanded breakfast. The cook gave him a long look,
then pointed to the coffeepot and a frying pan with
some meat in it which he had left near the fire. Harrison cut off a piece of meat and put it in his mouth.
He spat it out.

"It's cold!" he shouted to the cook. "I want it
hot."

Sudden as a tornado, the cook, who was a little
man, started to shower the contents of the chuck
wagon on the six-foot-two Harrison. Tin mugs,
knives, forks, spoons, tin plates, meat, potatoes all
rained down on the stupefied Harrison. These mis-

siles were accompanied by a series of oaths screamed
in incoherent rage.

Harrison backed off and said loudly to the smirk-
ing onlookers as he went to get his saddle, "I've a
mind to plug the dirty little skunk, except you'd all
expect me to cook if I did away with him."

The men exchanged knowing looks, aware that a
day's riding on an empty stomach would make Harrison more punctual for breakfast in the future.

The cattle bellowed and stirred up dust as they
jostled around. They were ready to move. Another
day had begun.

The forward man came back that day with news
that the Snake River was ahead, and a day later they
all saw the broad stretch of water in the distance. The
herd would reach it by late afternoon. Harrison and
Cluskey rode in advance to pick a crossing place and
told Aimesley to hold back the animals from the
river. They had had no water since the previous day
and might run out of control if they neared the river,
plunge in, and drown.

When Harrison and Cluskey reached the riverbank, what they saw up close looked even worse
than it had from a distance. The river was about a
quarter mile across. The water was high from snow
meltoff; it was muddy and churned in boils and
eddies. There was no way they could cross it here.
They rode downstream and, after rounding a bend,
saw a ferry in operation. It was a flat-bottomed scow
attached to a steel cable that stretched over the water
from bank to bank. A man operated a tackle that ran
through pulleys to bring the craft toward the bank
they were on, and they rode down to where the cable
was anchored in the bank. Besides the man, the scow
carried two attached freight wagons, a team of eight

oxen, and their drover. The ferry was far too small to be of any use to their herd, but it was likely that the ferryman would know of a fordable crossing.

"I'll show you where to put them in the water and where they can come out after they swim across," the boatman volunteered, "but it'll cost you fifty cents a head. You need to find a place where the bank shelves gradually down to the water for them to go in, and the same thing on the Idaho side for them to clamber out safely. I'll have to hire four men and two boats to help me, but that's included in the price. How many head have you?"

Cluskey beat him down from a half dollar a head to five cents per animal and said the herd would get in late in the afternoon.

"That's fine," the ferryman said. "By then the sun will be behind their backs. They won't swim with the sun in their eyes because they can't see where they're going from the glare on the water. And don't give them nothing to drink. When the water's this high, they won't go in the river unless they have a ten-thousand-dollar thirst."

Harrison asked him in a doubtful tone, "You think the cattle will make it across in a flood like this?"

"You'll lose some, without a doubt," the ferryman replied. He didn't seem too concerned at the prospect.

After they had ridden away, Harrison said to Cluskey, "Half those cows were paid for with my cash. I'm damned if I'll sit by and see them washed away. I say we don't take them across the Snake."

"All right," Cluskey said, surprising Harrison with his agreeableness. "We can camp here and wait for the waters to go down. It shouldn't take more than a month."

That was the end of that conversation.

* * *

The cattle moved through the sagebrush, bellowing with thirst. As they neared the river, they smelled
the water and built up speed, the stronger beasts dis-
tancing themselves out front from the others, so that
the herd became strung out in a long procession. The
cowhands rode on the flanks, hardly needing anyone
now to bring up the rear. Harrison and Cluskey had
ridden ahead again and met with the ferryman, who
showed them where to drive the cattle into the river.

"Keep them cows moving until they're all in the
water," he told them. "While they're swimming, I'll
ferry some of your men across to meet them on the
far side." He pointed downriver to where the cattle
would gain ground on the far side.

The point of entry into the water was about a half
mile above the ferry cable, and the landing on the far
bank about a half mile below it. This meant that the
herd would be carried by the currents about a mile
downstream while crossing the turbulent river a
quarter mile wide. Even Cluskey had to silently share
a look of doubt with Harrison—with whom he never
normally agreed these days—and he refused to pay
the ferryman anything in advance.

"Where are the four men with boats you said you
were hiring?" Cluskey wanted to know.

"They're in place," the ferryman said. "You just
get the beeves in the water here."

Harrison and Cluskey rode back and pointed the
herd leaders toward that section of riverbank. The
longhorns had broken into a clumsy trot, and nothing
could have stopped them from getting to the river
now, save black powder explosives or a pack of
wolves. The ground shook as they rumbled in a long
dusty train to slake their desperate thirst. They half
ran, half skidded down the incline to the river, and

the first ones in just pointed their heads upstream and
let the water flow into their mouths.

All hands got behind the rest of the herd and
roared and hollered in order to drive them into the
river. The cattle behind pushed those in front into
deeper water, where they had to swim. They turned
their heads around and tried to swim back to shore.
At this moment, two skiffs emerged from the tall
reeds along one part of the bank. In each craft, one
man rowed while another banged pots and pans and
shouted. The cattle had never seen anything like
them before. They turned around once more and
began to swim for the opposite shore. Once the
leaders were under way, it was not much trouble to
drive the rest of the herd after them. As they moved
out into the deeper water, the currents began to
sweep them downstream.

Cluskey and Harrison took their horses up on a
high section of the riverbank opposite the landing
place on the Idaho side. They were well downstream
of the swimming herd and watched the ferry cross
with three of their men and their mounts, who would
meet the cattle on the far side. The flat-bottomed
scow was in midstream when Harrison noticed that it
had stopped moving and that the ferryman was desperately pulling at the tackle and pulleys attached to
the cable. Upstream from the now stationary scow, a
huge raft of horned heads was floating down steadily.

The men on the ferry were beyond shouting distance, but they saw their predicament soon enough.
Two rushed to help the ferryman with the tackle.
Cluskey and Harrison said nothing as they watched,
knowing what those men felt trapped there in an advancing sea of longhorns. The cattle could not control their own movements well enough to avoid the
craft. Once some hit it, others would plow into them
and the boat from behind—until the wood boat was

splintered into pieces and floated downstream in fragments among the struggling steers.

The ferryman and two of the men worked desperately. The third man seemed paralyzed with fright. They got the scow moving again and cleared out of the way of the advancing horns with not many yards to spare.

Neither Cluskey nor Harrison made any remark later about the ferry's close call, having learned that the daily physical risks faced on the frontier were forgotten as soon as possible rather than discussed. An incident that would have kept a New Yorker in dinner conversation for months was deliberately put out of mind after a few minutes out here. The only thing they heard from the men at the camp fire that night, with the herd safely on the Idaho bank, was from one hand: "I don't swim, so I reckon I'd have walked ashore across the backs of them cows." They let it go at that.

The easiest way for them to go was to follow the Oregon Trail backward toward its source. This trail more or less followed the course of the Snake River southeastward, but the land was bare of grass, farmers had fenced off many areas, and settlements had sprung up along the way. They needed open rangeland where the grass had not already been gnawed to the roots by hungry animals passing through. To the south of the Snake River there were mountains and canyons. Cluskey persuaded them that the best route would be due east, straight across southern Idaho to Fort Hall, then south from there. Of the three, Jimmy Cluskey was the only one who troubled to ask around for advice from everyone he met who looked as if he knew what he was doing. So they all agreed they should head for Fort Hall.

Ada and Elmore counties were good cattle-buying

territory. The land was hard and mean, and those who scraped a living from it were glad to part with their stock for instant payment in gold coins. In a few days they doubled the size of the herd and had to send twice by stage for special shipments of coin from their banks. They hired more cowpunchers to run the herd east all day while they were out buying. At the end of the day the herd was not hard to find, and it was usually not as many miles farther on as if they had stayed to set the pace. But there was no point in forcing the steers now. They had a long journey ahead of them, through areas of lava beds where water and grass might be scarce. The longhorns would need their strength then and could not be tired by hard driving at this stage.

John Harrison worked out his own method. He spent the day drinking and playing cards in whatever little towns they came across—and most were no more than a collection of shacks and tents. That way he heard about who needed money and had beeves to sell. It kind of pissed off Cluskey and Aimesley, who had to do the work of tallying and branding, but it was the fastest way to get information. For every cattleman Cluskey and Aimesley heard about, Harrison heard about six at the gaming tables or at the bar. He even won some beeves playing faro.

They were getting on better with Harrison since he was able to spend time entertaining himself. It did a lot for his mood. Aimesley and Cluskey stole a few hours in saloons too. The long hard drive, lasting for weeks, was harder for them to take mentally than physically. Day after day they listened to roaring cattle lumbering along over dusty plains. Dust in their eyes, dust in their mouths and up their nose, baked by the sun, sore from the saddle, stiff from sleeping on the ground, irritated at one another and at their hired hands, they pushed on and on. Of the three, only Cluskey didn't wonder why he was doing this. He knew. But Aimesley and Harrison could have been doing a hundred other more pleasurable things. They weren't doing this for the money. They were doing it to show their families—and themselves— that they were grown men. By now both suspected that there must be a lot of easier ways to prove this, but things were too far gone to back out at this stage.

"Cluskey tricked us into this," Harrison liked to say from time to time to Aimesley. "He's the only one who benefits. When the drive is over, he'll have money, while he had none before. He's using us."

"He's not trying to cheat us, John," Aimesley said. "He's honest, and that's what counts with me. We thought Cluskey knew more than either of us, and so we were using him, too."

"Now we see that he is just as foolish as we," Harrison commented.

"Maybe tougher, too."

It annoyed Harrison to have Aimesley defend Cluskey. Before they came out west, Aimesley would never have dared to differ openly with him. Harrison could not figure out what had come over Aimesley to make him behave like this.

When Cluskey and Aimesley rode into Mayfield, in Elmore County, after having spent the morning unsuccessfully searching for cattle to buy, they were surprised to find Harrison in none of the saloons. Mayfield wasn't much of a town, and its saloons were dirty makeshift huts, some with earth floors and canvas roofs, but it was the only town and these were the only saloons within a day's ride of the herd. He had to be here someplace. In a back room with some sporting woman. Or in some high-stakes card game behind a curtain for privacy. But they couldn't find him, and no one had seen him around. Cluskey and

Aimesley soon forgot about him as they became distracted by what Mayfield had to offer.

They'd both had a few drinks in Sawtooth Kate's when two good-looking girls pushed in through the batwing doors. They ignored the whistles and hoots which met their arrival, brushed aside one drunk who'd spent all his money anyway on white lightning, and picked their way across the saloon floor with pretty little steps in their French silk gowns, with an air of innocence—as if they were at a church picnic. They sat together at a table and pretended to be too intrigued with each other's conversation to bother looking around to see who was in the saloon.

"Come on," Cluskey said to Aimesley, who shyly followed him across to the table at which the women were sitting. "My friend here, name of Winthrop," he said to the ladies, "was talking about buying some champagne."

"I was?" Aimesley asked in genuine surprise.

The women laughed. One said, "Winthrop, there ain't no such thing as champagne in this town. Change that to gin. At least they don't make it locally, like they do that whiskey you boys been drinking."

Jimmy Cluskey carried the talk with the women without much help from Winthrop Aimesley. Winthrop passed from being too shy to talk to being too drunk to talk without ever going through a talkative phase. Jimmy was glad to leave after a little while with the auburn-haired, shapely one with the mild manner and leave Winthrop with the blonde, equally shapely, with the sharp tongue.

She took Jimmy back to her cabin. Although the place was constructed of rough-hewn, unpainted timbers carelessly hammered together and didn't look like much from the outside, inside it was decorated in a feminine style, with pink fabrics hanging on the walls and a white carpet on the floor. Jimmy kicked off his boots and left them outside the door, so he wouldn't dirty the place up.

As he watched, she slipped out of her silk gown and took off her stockings and her underclothes. Then she sat naked at her dressing table, looking in the mirror as she brushed her hair. He looked at her bare shoulders, her back narrowing sharply to her waist, the cleft of her buttocks, and the way the flesh of her buttocks flattened on the stool. He felt himself grow hard.

Jimmy quickly threw off his clothes, crossed the room, and stood behind her. Looking in the mirror over her shoulder, he guided his hands around her front to clasp her breasts. Her nipples stood on end, and he circled them with his fingertips, over the areolae of her breasts. Her body trembled in response to his caresses.

Then he let his stiff cock urgently poke her in the back. She stood willingly and went with him to the bed, where she lay back submissively and closed her eyes.

He mounted her, guiding his member inside her. As he pushed deep within her and heard her grunt with passion, Jimmy knew for sure that if he could get this every four days, he could drive a herd of beeves to hell and back.

"What's wrong with me?" the blonde demanded to know. "Why don't you want to come to bed with me?"

Winthrop took a long pull on his drink. He didn't feel drunk anymore all of a sudden, and now he was dreading a scene with this woman in the saloon. He hadn't even wanted to get into this. Cluskey had dragged him along.

"I'm tired," he said lamely.

"You stupid little bastard!" she screamed, causing the men at the bar to turn around to look and listen.

Winthrop cringed.

Her eyes flashed. "You sit here mumbling at me, wasting my time. You make me sick." She got to her feet as if she were going to flounce off, then seemed to change her mind, bent down, and looked him in the face. Her lips were wide in a sneer. "You know what's wrong with you?" she screamed. "You can't screw!"

Winthrop looked mortified. "My good lady—"

"Don't you 'lady' me, asshole." She lifted the weight of her breasts in her hands beneath the silk material of her gown and thrust them in his face. "Show me your hard-on. Come on. Let me see."

The men along the bar laughed and jeered.

Winthrop was so shocked, he could neither move nor get a word out.

Her hands were now on her hips, and she thrust forward her lower belly against the seated man's cheek. Her voice was soft and pleading. "Do it to me, Winthrop. Come on, do it."

The men at the bar were whooping and yelling.

She gyrated her hips. "Please, Winthrop, try and get it up for me."

He sat motionless, except for the twitching of his mouth, his face deadly pale.

No one hardly noticed the batwing doors swing in and John Harrison stride over to the table. He was fast on the uptake and saw that his friend was being given a bad time.

"Come here, honey," Harrison said to the woman in a friendly tone. "Leave him alone. I have a present for you."

He held out a large buckskin bag to her. She took the heavy bag and loosened the rawhide thong which bound its top. She peered curiously inside and screamed. Then she dropped the bag with a *thump* and ran out the door.

A silence fell on the saloon, and everyone heard the barkeep when he said, "Hell, I thought she'd seen just about everything there is to see and never blinked an eye so long as she was paid to look at it."

The men went back to their drinks—all of them wondering what was in that bag but no man wanting to show he was a busybody.

Harrison took a slug from the gin bottle on Winthrop's table and then carefully poured two large measures into empty glasses. He put one in front of himself and the other next to him. He picked up the bag, reached inside, and pulled out a long tangle of jet black hair. Hanging at the end of the hair was the severed head of an Indian warrior.

Harrison tried to stand the head on the table in front of the glass of gin, but he had to prop it upright with a bottle against one ear.

Winthrop's chair crashed as he fell backward in a dead faint.

CHAPTER FOUR

Two of the five other Pinkertons who had been hunting down Mad Harry Clark on the Quinn River in northern Nevada were assigned with Raider on his new case. He hadn't bothered previously to take a close look at either of them, choosing instead to strike out on his own. Now he looked them over and he didn't like what he saw. One was sharp and shifty, and Raider thought of him as a clerk. Raider was convinced that the Pinkerton Agency was becoming overrun with clerks, who spent so much of their time doing paperwork and observing petty regulations that they rarely got around to confronting badmen. The other Pinkerton was wide-eyed and dumb, and Raider thought of him as a farmboy. In Raider's view, the big difference between clerks and farmboys was that clerks thought themselves too smart to need to learn anything new, and farmboys were willing but so slow they were liable to cause everybody to be killed before the lessons sank in.

"Hell, I'm a farmboy myself, so I ought to know," he liked to say. "But I come from Arkansas, and you've heard what the goddamn Yankees done to us down there after the war. I got the hayseeds knocked out of my hair when I was still only a kid. But nowadays you get these big dumb shitkickers coming off farms straight into the agency. I don't know what Mr. Pinkerton has in mind, excepting maybe to hire them out to plow land."

Now here he was, stuck with a clerk and a farmboy, with orders to track down a pair of rich men's sons who had fallen in with bad company in Oregon. Raider was not looking forward to this. But he was a practical man. He would start at the beginning. By getting drunk and maybe frightening off the clerk and the farmboy. That didn't work. The clerk didn't drink, and Raider ended by having to save the farmboy from getting badly beaten up by some cowhands who had taken a dislike to him for some reason. Raider dragged the farmboy back to the hotel and went out again, hearing later that the farmboy beat up the clerk, having mistaken him for one of the cowhands. It was not clear to Raider why the clerk blamed him for this instead of the farmboy.

Now he had a hangover and was still stuck with both of them, while they waited for a stagecoach north at Rebel Creek, at the western edge of the Santa Rosas. All three had sold their horses but kept their saddles, intending to buy fresh horses up in Oregon when they found the trail of Winthrop Aimesley and John Harrison.

Raider had a dull pain in his gut and decided on a few beers for breakfast in a saloon, while his two Pinkerton partners loaded eggs, ham, and biscuits into themselves at an eating house along the street.

As he stood at the bar, he heard a coach came in and thought it was the northbound one at first. He was told that the northbound and southbound often met at Rebel Creek—in fact there was a competition among the drivers to see if one could clear the town before the other arrived. Raider watched them change the team of horses and unload and reload passengers and freight. He knew what he had to do.

When the driver climbed up on the stage and yelled his last warning that he was about to leave town, Raider shouted to him to wait a minute. He rushed into the eating house, rousted the two Pinkertons from their table before they had finished their meal, and bundled them outside before him. Raider carried their saddles, one on each arm, and threw them up to the man at the back of the coach. He pushed his two partners, along with their bags, inside the coach, slammed the door after them, and gave the driver the signal to go. The driver cracked his whip over the backs of the team, and the coach lurched forward on its way south out of town. With any luck, Raider thought, those two would be in Winnemucca before they realized something was wrong.

After going to the eating house and paying for the two men's meals, he returned to the bar for another beer. Already he was beginning to feel much better. He blamed the pain in his gut on the presence of the clerk and the farmboy rather than on the large quantity of bad liquor he had consumed the night before. Now that he'd gotten rid of them for a while, it was only natural that his stomach would be doing better.

Things hadn't been going too smoothly for him recently. Of course things never went smoothly for Raider, but of late they had been even rockier than usual. A lot of these troubles traced back to the time Doc Weatherbee quit the agency. Raider had had his share of quarrels with Doc—always on personal matters. When it came to working as partners, each had always known he could fully rely on the other. After Doc left to get married and settle down, in spite of Raider's warnings against such a risky undertaking, Raider had persuaded Wagner to let him work without a partner—only to be countermanded by Allan Pinkerton himself. Even Raider could not intimidate that big tough Scot.

His objections to the partners apparently foisted upon him at random by the Chicago office were not more grouchiness on Raider's part. In Pinkerton work, as in any law-enforcement duties, a man's life is often dependent on his partner's courage and abilities. Some of these agents they sent out west would have done fine back east but, in Raider's opinion, were not combat-hardened enough for the rigors of frontier life. In the East, a Pinkerton operative always had the force and majesty of the law behind him. Out west, too often he himself was the law, and he had nothing to back him up but quick wits and a fast gun.

As Raider saw it, desk-bound managers in Chicago headquarters who never had to put themselves at physical risk were needlessly endangering his life by sending him nervous halfwits as partners. If he was going to die on the job, he wanted it to be because he had been outsmarted and outgunned—not because some farmboy or clerk was still fiddling with his holster.

If someone had told him in the old days he was going to miss Doc Weatherbee bad, Raider would have laughed. But the plain and simple truth was that things hadn't been the same since Doc had gone. Weatherbee used to needle Raider and make him mad as hell—in fact Doc had a broken tooth in his mouth as a reminder of one time he hadn't moved fast enough out of the way of Raider's fist. However, the ways Doc had teased and annoyed him were now less strong in Raider's mind than all the ways he had been a trustworthy partner in dangerous situations. When one man saves another's life, it forges a special bond between them. Raider owed his life to Weatherbee many times. He doubted if he'd ever owe it to any of the clerks and farmboys being dumped on him these days.

He finished his beer when he heard the stagecoach pull in. Picking up his saddle and bag, he went outside. The steaming horses were being unharnessed and led from between the shafts. Raider passed up his saddle and bag to be stowed. A fresh team was being backed up to the coach. The driver shouted that he was late, there would be no delay, through passengers were to stay put or he'd leave them behind in Rebel Creek.

Raider opened the coach door and looked inside, hoping to see a pretty woman. Instead he saw the sour faces of his two Pinkerton partners.

The clerk said, "I'd heard stories about the lousy tricks you've pulled on others and I guessed you'd done the same to us. I got the driver to stop when he saw the other coach and we switched."

"Sure was a lousy trick," the farmboy said.

Raider closed his eyes and tried to sleep. He couldn't. The pain was back in his gut.

In New York, the grieving parents of Aimesley and Harrison received the first word of their sons' present whereabouts through a withdrawal they made on a bank in Burns. South of Poison Creek Summit, Burns was a town with forests and buttes to the north and west, and high desert to the east and south. Ranchers ran herds on open ranges in these drylands. Raider had been to Burns, and he told his two partners they weren't missing much by not going there. Aimesley and Harrison had gone southeast and made another withdrawal at a bank in Crane.

"This means they're running cattle now by this point, so they've really slowed down," Raider said, tracing a route with his forefinger on a map. "I reckon they took the trail to Venator, on the South Fork of the Malheur River, and then followed the river north. Anyway, they was last heard about in Juntura, which is near where the South Fork enters the Malheur. I'm betting that by this time they've been building themselves a herd and are beginning to think of driving east. They would've been buying bunches here and there and letting the main herd graze for a few days in one place while they traveled around. You can do that when your herd is still small and you can feed and water them with no problem. But when that herd gets large, them longhorns are like locusts—they eat all before them, and what they don't eat they trample into the dirt. You have to keep a big herd on the move to feed it and to stop it breaking into bunches that want to go in different directions."

The three men, the only passengers, peered at the map as best they could in the jolting stagecoach. The stage they had taken north had been bound for Burns. They had left it as it crossed the South Fork and took this one north along the river. Once they reached Venator, they would be following the actual route taken by Harrison and Aimesley. This made all three of them feel that at last they were getting someplace. It had been a long haul up from Nevada, across the parched land, past bleak bare mountains.

Raider had eased up on his two fellow Pinkertons, having decided that maybe they weren't so dumb after all, since they hadn't fallen for his wrong-way maneuver for very long. He realized that if he couldn't shake them loose, he might as well put them to use. They still didn't trust him, chewing over everything he said to them, trying to find a catch in it.

Raider was saying, looking at the map as best he could while it was being knocked around by the motion of the coach, "I guess they stuck with the Malheur east from Juntura as far as Harper anyways. That's about where they'd start in earnest on the drive east. I reckon we should buy horses and supplies at Juntura, since this coach line ends there. Harper is about a day's ride east."

"You reckon we're far behind them?" the farmboy asked.

"They drew that money out in Juntura three weeks ago. Riding a big herd, the most they could have made in that time would be two hundred miles. Probably a lot less. They had to cross the Snake River. I'd be surprised if we're more than five days' hard riding behind them. So long as we don't lose them."

"Or you us," the clerk said with a knowing smile.

"You think he still wants to dump us?" Calvin Lowry asked. He was the one Raider called the farmboy.

"If we give him half a chance," Philip Temple, the clerk, answered.

"So why not let him? We can find these fellas on our own."

They were talking together at a station while the horses were being changed. They had worked together in Illinois on some minor railroad cases. Both had looked forward to working with the legendary Raider of the Mad Harry Clark case, and both had been disappointed. They knew that in Raider's eyes they looked like fumbling weaklings. Neither kidded himself that he was of the same caliber as Raider, yet all the same, they felt he was treating them unfairly. They felt they deserved a chance to prove themselves. On the Quinn River, Raider had given them none. He had just cut out on his own and done the job with no help from anyone. It made everyone look bad back in Chicago, including Raider himself. Not that he gave a shit. They understood that.

Raider had been right about Calvin Lowry. He was a farmboy. He was big, with broad shoulders and thick arms. His brown tousled hair topped a face that was ugly as sin. The family farm was in southern Illinois. As the youngest of four sons, he didn't stand much chance of inheriting the farm. Since all the good land had been taken a generation ago in that part of the country, if he wanted to farm he would have had to move west to Nebraska or Iowa or even all the way to California or Oregon. Chicago was as far as he got. He knocked the gun from the hand of a bank robber there and got his name in the newspapers. Someone from the Pinkerton National Detective Agency came around to his lodging house next—the address was in the papers—and offered him a job.

He might look like a rube, but he had been around. He had worked the trains in Illinois and Missouri. He had been to Philadelphia once. Now he was pissed at Raider for the way he was behaving—like an adult stuck with two of someone else's children for the afternoon. First chance he got, he intended to show Raider how hard-bitten he was.

Raider was wrong about Philip Temple being a clerk. He was the son of a tailor in Chicago and had joined the Pinkertons straight from school. Although he was eighteen at the time, he looked only fifteen. Grown men dismissed him as a harmless kid, not caring what they said or did opposite him. When they found themselves looking down a gun barrel and heard him say he was a Pinkerton, some of them still could not believe it. When they saw his finger tighten on the trigger, they usually found it easier to believe him.

Phil had aged fast. By the time he was twenty, he looked his years. A Pinkerton's life was hard. He was thin. His chest was hollow, his skin pale, his hair lifeless, his shoulders stooped. Just to look at him, it would have surprised people to hear he had never known a day's sickness in his life and could make many a larger man cringe with his iron handshake. Also, he was smart. Most of his work had been in Chicago, Detroit, Toledo, Cleveland—he was clearly a city man. Therefore he was astonished when he heard he had been assigned to a case in Nevada. He later heard that somebody at head-quarters had decided he needed "rounding out" and so moved him from the streets to the desert with the stroke of a pen. He and Raider would have discovered that they had remarkably similar opinions about the agency managers, if they had ever gotten around to discussing it together, which wasn't likely the way things were going.

The first week in Nevada had been a disaster. Phil had never been on a horse before. The first couple of days, he spent almost as much time lying in the dirt as he did sitting in the saddle. But he stuck with it. He had no choice. Horseback was the only way of moving around in Nevada. Besides, even if a place was nearby, he hated to walk there because every place swarmed with rattlesnakes. Phil was secretly thankful that Raider had struck out alone and nailed Mad Harry without their help. Phil had struck out alone also, not to trap Mad Harry but to take riding lessons from a pretty schoolmarm who felt sorry for him. This was about the time he started enjoying frontier life.

* * *

Names didn't mean much in Juntura. Every man was Tom, Dick, or Harry, and no one inquired about last names. A man might be Tennessee Tom to tell him apart from German Tom or Tobacco Tom, but that was as far back in his family tree as it was polite to go. Last names were apt to appear on wanted posters in other states or to associate a man with one warring family in a Kansas feud—the kind of things a man wanted to leave behind when he came out west. So it was that no one could recall anyone by the names of Harrison or Aimesley.

Cal and Phil used photographs they had been given. The reactions were not good. When they asked men if they had seen either of the two people in these photographs, most hardly looked at the pictures, being much more intent on finding out who Phil and Cal were and why they were looking for anyone.

"We're their cousins," Phil said. "The families got together back east and sent us out here to plead with them to come home. Winthrop's mother is sick. John is needed to run the family store."

Even Phil himself admitted that this didn't sound very convincing, but once he had told this story to one man, he had to tell the same thing to others.

Raider wouldn't help them. He said he had to prepare for the long ride. When they asked him how he was going to prepare, he said he was going to get drunk and find a woman.

They knew Harrison and Aimesley were long gone from Juntura. The two would be out of Oregon, over in Idaho by now—but the young Pinkertons were ambitious and thorough. They were stuck in this town for the night, but they would have felt guilty just sloughing off, not putting their time to valuable use. There was always the chance someone would recognize those photographs and give them information they could use. So they kept on trying.

"I know that one there," one man said finally, pointing at Aimesley's picture. "I seen him in Harper. He was with someone—not the fella in this second picture here."

"We know who that was," Cal said. "Jimmy Cluskey is his name. We don't have a picture of him."

"What have you got these pictures for? Why are you after them?"

Phil told him his story about being cousins. They were at a bar in a saloon. Neither Pinkerton was drinking, but the tall, skinny man they were talking to was putting his whiskey away. His dirty yellow hair reached his shoulders, and he had cold blue eyes that had a crazy look to them.

"You two ain't bounty hunters?" he asked.

"No, I said we're cousins," Phil answered.

"Some fellas from back east get themselves the notion, when they're short of cash, that there's easy money to be made turning men in to the law," the tall man went on like he hadn't heard Phil. "Some man has a reward on his head—'wanted dead or alive'— you know how it goes. Now if you're bounty hunters, and I ain't saying that you are, I'm giving you fair warning about that fella you don't have the photo of—"

"Jimmy Cluskey."

"Yeah, him. I stopped him shooting a man in the back. Dirtiest, lowdownest thing I ever seen, and I seen plenty. So I saved the life of this critter from Cluskey, and you know what thanks I got? He turned on me. So I plugged him good. It was a fair fight. The marshal gave me no trouble over it. Everybody knows of me over in Harper. You ever go there, ask around about me. Tell them you met Yaller Dawg. Hell, yes, they know me."

"Mr. Dawg," Cal said earnestly, "when exactly did this incident take place?"

"I dunno. A while back."

Cal was using his Pinkerton training. "Think. When was it?"

"Why in hell should I think?" The cold blue eyes stared back at him. "If you ask me, you ain't no cousins of nobody. You look to me like a busybody. Maybe they done something wrong once and you're hounding them down because of it, not letting them start a new life. And you got me helping you. You sons-of-bitches is prying information out of me so you can hang two men."

Things were getting out of hand fast, so Cal put in quickly. "It's not like you think. So we're not cousins. It was dumb of us to tell you that. But the part about their families wanting them is the truth. They've done nothing wrong, at least that we know about. We're Pinkertons, sent to bring them home."

"You should've told me that in the first place," Yaller Dawg said.

"I guess so."

"Then I could have blown a hole in your head right off without being bothered talking to you."

Cal looked into those insane blue eyes and knew the man was serious. He said, "Why? I ain't done nothing to you."

"You Pinkertons gut-shot my brother. He took two days to die on the stone floor of a town jail. His buddy was put in the next cell, and he told us what happened before they hung him. Like they say about Injuns, the only good Pinkerton is a dead one."

Cal saw he had already said too much. He kept his mouth closed. His heart was pounding, his palms were sweaty, he wondered what was going to happen next. Phil was standing close by, not moving or saying anything either.

Yaller Dawg downed a half glass of straight whiskey. "I see you're wearing a Peacemaker, fella. I don't see nothing on your friend. I suppose he carries a pocket gun. Listen, I'm going to offer you two a square deal—which is more than you gave my brother. You and me is going to quick-draw, and may the best man win. Meanwhile your friend can go for his pocket gun, and I'm betting I get him as well as you."

Cal swallowed. He was still only learning to control the big Colt .45 he carried on his hip and hadn't even gotten around to thinking about fast draws. "That's mighty generous of you, Yaller Dawg," he said in a quavery voice, "but my friend Phil is a fast draw, and it would be plain dishonest to take you up on your offer."

Yaller Dawg looked at Phil in surprise. Cal belted him with his fist on the jawbone. Cal's big shoulders and brawny arm packed a mighty punch, but Yaller Dawg was edgy and fast, like all gunfighters. He saw the punch coming out of the corner of his eye and managed to move his head enough to avoid taking it full force. All the same, it knocked him to his knees on the saloon floor.

Cal jumped him and tried to yank Yaller Dawg's revolver from its holster while he was still stunned. Yaller Dawg slammed him in the nose, blinding him with pain and his own tears. Both men were on their knees on the sawdust. Yaller Dawg threw a right cross that caught Cal square in the mouth.

Phil came in with a boot to the tall man's ribs which made him howl like a stuck pig. But he didn't go down. Instead he climbed to his feet and went for his gun.

"Behind you!"

The sudden shout caused Yaller Dawg to spin around and draw as he went. He saw the man who had shouted this warning to him, a big man with a black mustache and black leather coat, standing in the saloon doorway. His hand was on his gun handle, like he was giving Yaller Dawg a chance to change his mind.

This was something Yaller Dawg hated to do, especially when he considered he had the advantage. He went to nail the stranger in the doorway. His gun barrel came up fast.

Yet it didn't move with the lightning speed of the long-barrel Remington .44 that his opponent brought to bear on him. This gun coughed smoke, and Yaller Dawg's face twisted in pain. His unfired six-gun dropped from his right hand, and his long, skinny frame swayed unsteadily. Then he came crashing down stiffly, like a sawn-through redwood.

Raider gave his two Pinkerton partners a kind of disgusted half-smile as he holstered his gun. He said, "I'll be in the bar next door if you boys need me."

CHAPTER FIVE

Cluskey said they badly needed more horses. "Those cheap nags we bought for six dollars apiece back in Oregon ain't holding up to a full day's herding, even though they're being rested for five or six days each time after being ridden. We'll be hiring more men in the next few days. They'll be needing horses too."

"I've been told that the Indians hereabouts have the best horses," Harrison said.

"You stay away from those Indians. They're liable to have heard about you cutting off that Bannock brave's head."

Harrison shook his head. "The band here, although they're Bannocks too, aren't friendly with those back there. Anyway that Indian was stealing my horse. I had a right to shoot him."

"You and me have talked about that subject long enough, and we didn't get anywhere. Don't bring it up again."

"You said to keep away from Indians," Harrison accused. "So far as I'm concerned, you're the one who brought up the subject. I'd kill a white man if he tried to steal my horse, not just an Indian."

"That's very evenhanded of you," Cluskey said. "Find out where these Indians are and if they want to sell horses. And make sure they're on good terms with white folks. I don't want my hair lifted."

A stockman told Harrison where to talk with some of the local Bannocks. He said they were peaceful and hadn't been involved in any of the troubles. He warned Harrison, however, that farther east the Bannocks and Shoshone were scattered in traveling war parties, laying waste wherever they went. The Indians that Harrison met agreed to sell him horses and told him where they would corral the animals next morning.

He, Cluskey, and Aimesley rode out next day after having got the herd moving. Horses being much faster than cattle, they could easily catch up to the herd later in the day with their new purchases. Cluskey for once was not feeling sure of himself. He had by now adapted his New York street cunning into the style of hard bargaining used by western ranchers and had proved himself a shrewd businessman. Dealing with Bannock warriors was going to be different. They wouldn't know much English, so he couldn't joke and kid along with them. Then there was the nagging thought that the Indians had no real intention of trading in horses, that this was a trap to avenge the warrior Harrison had shot and, in a moment of madness, beheaded.

They rode in a line on a narrow trail that twisted among barren hills. Aimesley was last. He shouted, "Hey, we have company."

The others turned in the saddle and looked back. A mounted Indian made a fourth in their line. His chest was bare, he wore buckskin leggings, and he used a blanket instead of a saddle. His brand-new Winchester repeater's stock was decorated with beadwork. He nodded to them pleasantly, apparently pleased by the impression his unnoticed arrival had made on them.

"You think he's alone?" Aimesley asked, unable to keep the fear out of his voice.

"Why don't you ask him?" Harrison joked.

"Pull over and let him by," ordered Cluskey, who was in front.

They did. The Indian passed Aimesley by without a glance at him, but when he came alongside Harrison he reined in his horse. He spent a few moments looking over Harrison's mount rather than Harrison himself. Aimseley and Cluskey's mounts were ordinary cayuses, but Harrison had treated himself to a magnificent black stallion, for which he had paid a hundred dollars.

The Indian pointed to the horse and nodded his appreciation. "How much?" he asked.

Before Harrison could say anything, Cluskey put in, "Ten dollars."

Harrison just kind of choked with rage.

The Indian just nodded and urged his horse along the trail ahead of them. He rounded a bend. When they came to that point, he had disappeared. There was no sign of him, although they could see a quarter mile down the trail from there.

Harrison was grumbling about Cluskey's attempt to sell his horse for a ludicrous price, and Aimesley was complaining that they were surrounded by hostile savages and would never be seen alive again by white men—or white women, for that matter.

Harrison jibed at him: "Winthrop, maybe they'll make you their blood brother, give you the chief's daughter, and let you lead them on raids."

Even Winthrop found that funny. "If they do, John, I guarantee you a slow death."

Before leaving New York, Harrison and Aimesley had read accounts of Indian life and seen paintings of warriors. They had both looked forward to seeing such picturesque braves on their journey and had been disappointed by those few Indians they had seen so far, who had been hangers-on at the edge of cow towns. This one, although not attired in ceremonial regalia, had been much more like what they had been hoping to see.

Cluskey, on the other hand, had been convinced that Indians were demonic, maybe only half human, and certainly cannibals. The fact that Harrison had cut the head off an Indian upset Cluskey because he thought his friend had behaved like one in doing it, while Aimesley was shocked because he knew Harrison had no excuse desecrating a dead body and probably very little for shooting him in the first place, even if the Indian was a horse thief.

Of all three, Cluskey had been the most deeply fearful before setting out to trade horses with these Bannocks. Now he was suddenly confident, ignoring their comments, even whistling in his annoyingly tuneless way as he led them along the trail.

"Does trying to sell my horse for a few dollars make you feel that good, Jimmy?" Harrison asked.

"I knew he wasn't going to buy," Cluskey said. "They probably traded their horses for goods before, and so they don't know how much their horses are worth in dollars. They sent that brave down to find out. If they think a horse like yours is worth only ten dollars, we should get some bargains from them. If we'd asked a hundred and fifty, you can imagine the prices we'd be asked. Them Bannocks are pretty sharp. Give them a day or two and they'd do all right in New York."

* * *

Give or take fifty, they had twenty-two hundred beeves moving across Idaho, a huge moving carpet of hide and horns that raised a column of dust behind that rose high in the air and could be seen for miles.

"Well, Jimmy, I have to admit to you," Aimesley said, "I could never have imagined a sight like this, least of all with me in it. I have to thank you for bringing me out here."

Cluskey shrugged. "What makes you think I ever imagined it either? I've seen a lot of people teeming on the East Side streets in New York, but that's all. Give me longhorns anytime—especially if they're on their way to market."

The three were watching the herd move out before they went off to buy new bunches up ahead, which they would join with the main herd later in the day. A rancher they had met the previous day told them that his small spread and some others lay in a valley to the southeast. He would expect them to come by and look over what he had to sell. To make the trip worth their while, he would get his neighbors to bring in some stock also. It took them a long while to find their way to the valley, and they realized they were going to have a hell of a time driving the cows out. They thought about giving up and going back to the herd a few times, but almost out of habit by now they persisted.

They ended buying a little over two hundred head from four ranchers, paid them in gold, and gratefully accepted the offer of their help in driving the beeves partway back with them. Once they got the animals past a system of gullies through a low range of hills, they could follow the bed of a dried-up stream which would bring them close to where they expected the herd would be. The ranchers would go as far as the streambed with them.

Coming off four separate ranches, the cattle were unused to being together and did not run naturally in a single group. Also, they were coming fresh off grass and had plenty of energy to waste on fun and games. These longhorns were more or less wild, since they had only been rounded up once before— and that had been as calves to be separated from their mothers, branded, and castrated. If they had any memory of that event, it wasn't making them any easier to handle now.

The men sweated under the hot sun as they urged their horses this way and that to cut off mutinous steers and galloped after those that succeeded in breaking away. It was hard work, but things were going reasonably well until they came to the gullies. Here the four ranchers who were helping them suddenly seemed to find great difficulty in heading off bolting animals. Chasing after them without cutting them off only made the steers run harder. The animals split up into small groups and ran in all directions, further panicked by the curses and yells of the ranchers.

"The bastards are breaking them up on us!" Harrison yelled. "They know their cattle will find their way back to their home grass, so they'll have their animals back and our gold in their pockets. Damn them, I'll see them six foot under before they rob me!"

He pulled his rifle from its saddle scabbard and loosed off a bunch of shots at the ranchers. This made them quit scattering the cattle and ride for safety.

"Let them go!" Aimesley shouted.

But Harrison wanted vengeance. He selected one man and carefully drew a bead on him. He fired three times before knocking off the rancher's horse. When the man picked himself up off the ground and began running, Harrison spurred his horse and cantered forward, clearly intending to run him down.

"Fuck him!" Cluskey yelled after Harrison. "Come help us round up whatever beeves we can. That's what's important." When Harrison ignored him and rode on with a murderous look on his face, Cluskey shouted to Aimesley, "Stop him, Winthrop!"

Although Aimesley had an inferior horse, he was much lighter in the saddle than Harrison, and he was by far the better horseman. He pulled alongside Harrison's mount, then used his horse to shoulder into Harrison's and break its stride. When his horse came to a stop, Harrison's face was twisted and his hands shook in fury. It seemed as if he might use the rifle on his friend for having thwarted him. It was only with difficulty that he managed to control himself.

Aimesley said quietly, "We need you to help round up what cattle we can."

They worked hard at it and brought together about seventy of the more than two hundred head they had paid for. When they had them running nicely beyond the gullies, by the side of the dry steambed, Aimesley took the opportunity to have a few private words with Harrison.

He said, "Back in New York, Jimmy Cluskey was the wild one. Out here he's grown calm and hardworking. In the city, we two were such proper gentlemen we changed our clothes three times a day and wore gloves to read newspapers so we wouldn't get our hands dirty. I can't say how I've changed out west, but I can say that a cruel, bloodthirsty streak has emerged in you which I never observed in you before." When Harrison avoided his eyes and said nothing in reply, Aimesley continued, "It's not for the money you wanted to kill that rancher, John. Jimmy is here for the money—unlike us—and even he said that it was even-Steven the way we cheated the Bannocks and then the ranchers cheated us.

They had bought thirty horses, worth thirty to fifty dollars apiece, for ten dollars each, the price Cluskey had originally quoted the Indian on the trail for Harrison's stallion.

When Harrison still said nothing, Aimesley asked him, "How are you going to settle down again back in polite society if you let yourself go like this?"

"I'm *never* going back to New York."

Aimseley was puzzled and disturbed by the intense look in Harrison's eyes and the vehemence in his voice as he said this.

From time to time they hit a plentiful supply of good grass and sweet water, and in these places they gave the herd, and themselves, a day's rest. The cattle ate the fresh grass nonstop and swallowed down water until the fermenting liquid inside them caused their sides to swell. A few always died. The rest put on weight and changed from tired, bony, drooping creatures to frisky, quarrelsome longhorns again.

When there was no town nearby, the three rode separately short distances away in order to have some time by themselves. The cowhands thought this was just fine anywhere else, but not in Bannock country. They didn't wander far from camp, wishing, as they said, to keep the hair on their heads. If know-nothing Easterners thought they could stroll about Idaho as if it were a city park, good luck to them.

After they had come in the late afternoon to one grassy place by the edge of a pond and decided to rest the next day there, Cluskey took a ride by himself. It was a couple of hours before sundown, and he reckoned he had time to get away by himself for a while. He rode his horse over a hill covered with a few scraggly pines and went down the other side, just so he could no longer see the beeves or hear their lowing. The world seemed to him suddenly to be a fresher, pleasanter place, now that he could no longer see a single steer.

Cluskey was startled to hear a stone kicked by a horse's hoof. He grabbed his revolver and snapped back the hammer.

"Hey there, young fella, take it easy. I ain't no Injun or desperado." The man talking looked like he was nearly sixty. He was small, wiry, and dried-up-looking from the sun. His horse looked the same. "You one of the fellas with that big herd eating my sheep grass?"

"This is open range, mister."

"Reckon so. All the same, I was hoping to have it all to myself. Not much competition round these parts. Me and my two brothers run two big flocks. We've got sixty thousand sheep, all told. I'm on my way from one to the other right now. I'm coming back this way tomorrow. Thought I might ask you what news you bring. Been two months since any of us has talked to someone from outside."

Cluskey was familiar with this appetite for news and gossip on the part of men he would have thought apart from all that. Yet he found that the wildest-looking mountain man wanted to hear all about New York, all about anything—even some row in a distant small town where he had never been. Cluskey swore to himself that as soon as the lonely wilderness made him this desperate, he would head back east in a hurry. Meanwhile he enjoyed having such close attention paid to his stories and opinions—something Cluskey hadn't experienced before. The talk went from politics to women and from women to horses.

"I saw your remuda," the sheepherder said. "You've some nice animals there. Why don't you ride one of them instead of that nag there?"

This stung Cluskey, because he happened to be riding his favorite horse. "You call that flea-bitten bag of bones you're riding a horse? Hell, with all that long hair, except for its size, I'd have sworn it was a burro. It ain't a mule, is it?"

"This dang horse would leave yours a hundred yards behind over a quarter mile," the sheepherder boasted.

"I'd take you on if I didn't think the poor thing would die in the middle of it."

"All right, New York, I've heard your talk, now let me see your money." The sheepherder reached in the pocket of his sheepskin jacket and, to Cluskey's surprise, pulled out a fistful of gold coins.

Cluskey reached in his own pants pocket and produced a single ten-dollar gold piece. It was all he had in the world.

"That's all you think of your horse?" the sheepherder jeered.

"I ain't in the habit of carrying large sums with me when I take a ride in the hills," Cluskey said. He added sarcastically, "It's not often I come across sporting gents with racehorses in the back of beyond."

His sarcasm was lost on the sheepherder. "Ten dollars it is, then, though it's been a long time since I exerted myself for such a small sum." The sheepherder selected a ten-dollar piece, and, after putting the rest of the gold back in his pocket, he placed the coin on a rock.

Cluskey set his coin beside it. From the sheepherder's attitude, he should have been worried—but no man with a fresh, healthy horse could feel threatened by the scrawny, ungroomed, loping animal that formed the competition.

They selected a quarter-mile stretch reasonably free of holes and rocks. The sheepherder allowed

Cluskey to count off the start and even gave him a bit of a lead to begin with. Just as Cluskey was beginning to feel good, the sheepherder's nag breezed past him, its long hide hair flying and its long splay legs eating up the ground. Cluskey was beaten with just about a hundred yards to spare.

That ten dollars he lost meant a lot to him. Aimesley and Harrison allowed him a hundred dollars a month. It was amazing how fast that could go having a high old time in a cow town. Although Cluskey handled thousands of dollars in purchasing steers, Aimesley had displayed a talent for bookkeeping and kept track of every dime. Uncaring about large sums of money in many ways, both Aimesley and Harrison had a kind of perverse stinginess about small cash amounts. They were quite likely to blow a hundred dollars on French champagne and refuse him a loan of five dollars. They said they felt he was taking advantage of their generosity.

"You said you were coming back this way tomorrow?" Cluskey asked.

"I sure am."

"You saw our remuda. You think that half-buffalo of yours can handle them?"

"If your friends have money."

"They sure have," Cluskey said with a grin.

When he arrived back at camp, he told everybody about the crazy man with the shaggy horse who said he could beat anything they had. The men were wary and told stories about being tricked by thoroughbred racehorses got out to look like cayuses. But when the sheepherder arrived next day and they got a look at the challenger, they laughed and dug deep into their pockets.

They ran four races, with the sheepherder's horse facing five fresh horses in each race. Aimesley rode in two of the races, coming in third in one. The challenging horse won the first three races and lost the fourth, as it tired. The sheepherder covered most bets, ranging from a couple of dollars with the cowhands to three pieces of twenty with Aimesley and Harrison. Those he didn't cover were taken by Cluskey, who cleared eighty dollars on three wins and a loss.

A wind sprang up shortly before sundown. Maybe this was making the cattle uneasy, or maybe it was just all the fresh grass and water and a day's rest. Four men were needed, instead of the usual two, to ride around the herd, as they refused to bed down for the night. The cook washed out his pots and pans after the evening meal. The wrangler tied a string of horses close to camp, seeing as how they might be needed in a hurry during the night. The restlessness of the steers made the men jumpy too, and they wondered what it was that the longhorns smelled on the wind—maybe wolves or a mountain lion.

At the camp fire, two men made saddle sheaths for their rifles from fresh rawhide. They took a strip of green rawhide about sixteen inches long and half as wide and cut a slit at each end. They slipped the slit at one end over a saddle horn, then wrapped the rawhide tightly around the rifle stock just over the lock, slipping the other slit over the saddle horn. As the rawhide dried, it would get stiff and assume the shape of the rifle. This kind of sheath or sling would hold a rider's piece snugly in front of him, hard to lose and easy to draw.

The beeves refused to lay down until it was pitch dark, and even then they constantly stirred and sparred among themselves. When Cluskey and a cowhand took their turn at watch, the steers had already stretched and turned over on their other side. It was near one in the morning, and Cluskey decided that two men could handle things instead of four. The cows were still uneasy but had caused no real trouble up till this point. He and the hand circled the herd in opposite directions, the cowboy singing slow sad songs, and Cluskey, unable to sing, whistling off-key.

The stars were huge overhead, and they could see well enough by their light to find their slow way around. Wolves were howling far off in the hills; now and then they heard the sharp bark of a fox nearby. When they first took the herd into Bannock country, these small yelps and cries at night used to make Cluskey sweat, because he knew that Indian warriors imitated them to communicate with one another during a night attack. Now he no longer worried about what he couldn't see—he had enough real problems in front of his eyes to blot out ones he might imagine.

"Think we might have a surprise party tonight," the cowhand said as he passed Cluskey on his round. "Them critters has gone awful still."

For a moment Cluskey thought he was talking about fox barks and Bannock warriors creeping up on them, then he realized that the man was talking about the longhorns. It was true, they had grown very quiet. Maybe they were finally settling down to rest. But Cluskey respected this hand's opinion. He was more experienced than any of them and seemed to have a sixth sense about longhorns.

Things were so quiet, in the darkness Cluskey could hear the wind blow through the grass. He heard a steer bawl, then suddenly the earth trembled beneath his horse and he heard the clash of horns as they struck against each other in the wild stampede.

Cluskey couldn't even be sure if they were coming his way. When he didn't get trampled into the dirt after a few seconds, he knew they weren't. He didn't have to rouse the men from their sleep to come help. The thunder of the steers' hooves did that. The horsemen all galloped into the darkness as blindly as the cattle, their horses stumbling when they hit uneven ground.

The herd had broken into three main bunches and slowed to a run, then finally to a puzzled halt, ready to stampede again if something spooked them. All hands spent the night riding around them, calming them down, shouting to one another to reveal their positions. They spent all night at this, while the cattle lowed uneasily and stamped their hooves.

At first light, they rounded the three bunches into one herd again and brought them to water.

"Sons-of-bitches won't want to move today because they been going all night," Cluskey said to Harrison. "We're missing some, too. It'd be hard to tell with this many head, except some of the leaders is gone. That mean one, and those two with the big spreads that's always together and pushing the others around."

Harrison agreed that these animals, which they all knew, were missing. "But that's all," he said.

One hand reckoned about a hundred head were gone. There was no sure way to tell, but the herd did seem slightly smaller. They were having breakfast and allowing the cattle a last chance to graze on the lush grass at this place when they saw a plume of dust raised by some moving cows.

Cluskey said, "Load your rifles, boys, and let's look."

They rode out and found a bunch of cattle moving toward them. They eased to the side and watched the expert way a single horseman controlled them, about seventy head. He ran his horse from side to side, did some yelling, and mysteriously the cattle went the way he sent them.

Aimesley said, "I thought we had got pretty good at this until seeing this man. You know, we don't know what we're doing."

No one argued with that.

Owing to the dust, they couldn't get a good look at the man who was driving the cows. They spotted their road brand on the front animals and then saw the leaders they had missed. When they finally saw the rider clearly, he turned out to be a scrawny man with white whiskers and an old muzzle-loader on his back, seated on a scrawny horse.

"If he wants to race us, the answer is no," Harrison said. "I don't care how bad his horse looks." He had lost heavily the previous day.

"I just picked up these strays back there in the hills," the rider shouted. "I was coming this here way, and I thought I'd bring 'em along. I allowed mebbe you'd have use for 'em. My name's Bob. That's my horse's name too, so folks gets us mixed up."

"We're mighty grateful," Cluskey said. "You know this country, Bob?"

"Better than them buzzards do. Still don't help me find gold, though. I reckon I'll try again farther east."

"We could use someone who knows the lay of the land. We'd pay two bucks a day and all you can eat come chow time."

Bob scratched his whiskers and thought for a while. "I reckon a man who knows these parts should get three dollars."

"You got it."

"But I'll leave just as soon as I get the notion there's gold in some damn hill."

"Fair enough," Cluskey said. "When you go, we'll stake you with beef and a sack of beans."

CHAPTER SIX

For half an hour every Sunday morning, Fletcher's Gold Star Saloon in the town of Harper was converted to a church. This kind of took some drinkers by surprise—visitors to town, unfamiliar with the custom. Their bottles and glasses were taken from them and put to one side, where they would be safe till after the service. If a man didn't like it, he could pay for his drinks and go elsewhere, but never show his face in the Gold Star again.

Raider didn't take too kindly to having his bottle confiscated, but when he heard the voice of the clergyman, he changed his mind. Preacher Hanrahan had a down-home Arkansas accent, and it did Raider good to hear the kind of talk they had in his home state. The preacher was a believer in fire and brimstone. He promised each and every one of them, if they did not repent in time, a fairly hot time in the next world. All this did to Raider was give him a terrible thirst.

When it came to collection time, two big, mean-looking hombres took their Stetsons off and stuck them in front of everyone. The way they scowled and kept their gun hands free, it came pretty close to a holdup. Contributions were generous.

Once the service was done, the preacher stayed for a few drinks with his parishioners. Raider poured him a stiff one from his bottle, and they remembered how things used to be in Arkansas. Raider had something on his mind too, something that had been puzzling him.

"I'm looking for two young fellas—I'm a friend of the family, you see—both decent kids. They hail from New York. I was kind of surprised when folk here in Harper said one of them—John Harrison—had killed a man in a card game. They said the marshal made Harrison pay for his burial, and also that they hired you to say prayers, which he didn't have to do. I know that Harrison is a good kid, and I thought you might have heard what caused this to happen. People often tell things to clergymen they don't say to others."

"I remember John. He caught a gambler named Frank Lime cheating. He shot him in cold blood. At that table over there."

"That's more or less what the others said," Raider acknowledged.

"Come with me." The preacher led Raider out a back door, and they walked up a little hill behind the saloon without speaking. At the top there was a small graveyard, surrounded by a picket fence to keep wolves and coyotes away. The preacher walked among the graves until he came to a pile of earth on which new grass and weeds had not yet grown. He pointed to an unpainted plank, hammered upright

into the ground at the head of the grave. On it was
written in pencil:

> Crooked cards and straight liquor,
> Slow horses and fast women,
> Lord have mercy on Frank Lime,
> Here he lies, before his prime.

Preacher Hanrahan asked, "You like that? Good.
Well, when you catch up with John Harrison, you tell
him I gave him his money's worth."

Raider and his two partners, the farmboy Calvin
Lowry and the clerk Philip Temple, found the ferryman who had helped Aimesley and Harrison's herd
to cross the Snake from Oregon eastward into Idaho.
They tracked them to the town of Mayfield without
much trouble. There they heard about Harrison putting the Indian's severed head on the table in front of
a glass of gin at Sawtooth Kate's.

"That wasn't all," a talkative storekeeper told
them. "The druggist took the head and pickled it in a
jar. Later, when Harrison was drunk, he went to the
druggist's, threatened the man at gunpoint, and shattered the jar containing the head with a bullet. He
scalped the head and left. The druggist put it in another jar of pickle. So far as I know, he's still got it,
and you can see it if you like."

Raider did. It wasn't a pretty sight, and the Pinkerton was surprised when the druggist tried to sell it
to him as a trophy.

"People in these parts are all crazy," Raider muttered and left the store, along with Cal and Phil. He
said to them, "Harrison seems to have gone loco out
here. I think it's all the influence of that little back-
shooting son of a bitch Cluskey, who persuaded them
to come out here and now has Harrison under his

power. When I catch up with them, I'll show Cluskey who's who. But that can wait. While we're in town, I reckon you boys will want to write up your reports for headquarters. Tell them I was asking for them, but too busy to send word."

While the two young Pinkertons dutifully kept to their hotel rooms in order to complete the reports upon which Chicago put such emphasis, Raider headed for the saloons.

He played some low-stakes faro until he became convinced that, as usual, this was not one of his winning days. He quit in time before he got stung. Mayfield whiskey tasted like it had been made in Mayfield, and not too long ago. Some good-looking ladies were around, and a big dance hall operated around the clock down the street. Raider wasn't much of a dancer, but then standards were not high in Mayfield. The men got fired up on corn liquor, paid their money, and it was up to their partners to avoid their boots and knees.

In Sawtooth Kate's a while later, he saw one of the women he had been dancing with. She told him she was a schoolteacher—only there were no schools and few children in these parts, so she had turned to dancing, since there was no shortage of lonely men. Except for kicked shins and trodden toes, she said it wasn't such a bad kind of life. Raider assumed she also did a little something else on the side—at least he hoped she did.

He remembered how Doc Weatherbee could always instinctively say the right thing to the ladies. Raider knew very well that he himself did not have this talent. He tried to be careful, he tried not to offend, stayed away from swear-words when he remembered, with the result that women found his talk dull when he was trying to impress them. Only when Raider relaxed and stopped trying to be careful about what he said, only then did he make a woman enjoy his company, because he too was enjoying himself. This was how he felt with this woman, and he only wished he could stay on in Mayfield for some days. But he had to ride on at first light next day, so he wasted no time.

He took her to his hotel room. He was surprised by her sudden shyness and assumed she was putting on an act. But when she went to unbutton his pants, he realized her shyness and awkwardness in the bedroom were genuine. She was no virgin, but she was no whore either. Her obvious inexperience in opening a man's pants excited him. When they had both stripped naked, she took his cock in her hand and pressed it between her legs. He rolled her over and spread her and thrust himself into her.

She gasped and cried out. He remained motionless inside her until her body relaxed beneath him and began to move in a pulsating rhythm. When she thrust herself strongly against him, he drove himself hard into her and pounded his hips against hers until he reached a heaving climax and drained his sperm into her.

They lay clinging tightly to one another on the bed until his erection returned. He was slower, gentler with her the second time.

The three Pinkertons were no more than a week behind the herd now, about two day's ride for them. Aimesley and Harrison were still buying bunches of cows along the way, forty here, sixty there, a hundred someplace else. They had to have close to three thousand head by now, which was a sizable herd by anyone's standards. The fact that two tenderfoot rich boys from New York had managed to put a herd this size together surprised Raider only a little less than the fact that they were keeping it together and moving east at a good pace.

The Pinkertons checked as they went, showing the photographs to ranchers who had sold them beasts, asking at stores in tiny towns where they might have bought supplies. There was no definite trail eastward, and big herds passed through only several times each year, so folk knew who they were. Three thousand longhorns are kind of hard to miss. Along some stretches, they could follow the path of the herd by the droppings and beaten-down growth. Other stretches, they left hardly a trace—and taking one wrong pass through the hills or one wrong stream valley could put them many more days again behind the herd.

"I'm no tracker," Raider warned his partners, "so you two keep your eyes peeled for signs of them."

"Unless they drop trolley car tickets, I'm not going to find them," Phil said. "I can tell one city street from another just by the look of the cobblestones, but this wilderness looks all alike to me, except for being rockier in some parts than others."

"Well, you can give me the clean dust out here any day instead of the filth of city streets," Raider said, provoking an argument about the relative merits of city and frontier life, which somehow got onto the War Between the States, with Raider making rebel yells and calling Phil a damn Yankee.

Cal just shook his head and laughed at them, knowing that neither one had been old enough to fight in that war.

They came across a rancher out riding his spread. Raider called to him. "You see a herd pass through this way maybe a week ago."

The rancher rode up to them with an unfriendly look on his face. "This is my land you're riding on. This ain't government rangeland."

"We'll try to stop our horses eating your grass, mister," Raider said with a grin, tipping back his hat.

The rancher looked at this big man a little more carefully and saw that, though he was smiling, he could not hide the air of menace about him. He decided that the two with him were greenhorns, and that all three were probably up to no good. He told them what they wanted to know, hoping to speed them on their way.

"That herd came by down that draw and made for water at the bottom of that hill. I had a bunch of steers out on grass and they got swept along with the herd. Me and two of my men took after them, but there was no way we could find our cows in that mob. The drovers all denied it, except one. He paid me for fifty head, though I think it was closer to seventy that got took up by their herd." He looked at the photos and picked Aimesley. "He's the one who paid me. Weren't for him, they would have picked me clean."

They rode on.

"Seems like our boys are learning all the tricks," Raider said. "Men have been known to snowball a small herd into a big one by running them through other men's cattle. Aimesley seems to be the only one of them fellas who still plays fair and square."

"He only paid for fifty head and the rancher said he took twenty more," Cal said.

Raider laughed. "Knowing ranchers, I'd guess Aimesley paid for twenty more than the herd actually swept off."

Raider knew he had the kind of appearance that made bank tellers nervous. The more casual he tried to be as he approached the teller's window, the more nervous the teller usually got. He solved this by letting Phil and Cal go into banks in the small towns

and ask if Harrison or Aimesley had made a withdrawal. They showed their Pinkerton identification
and normally had their questions answered. Banks
out here needed people like Pinkertons. They had to
be nice to them.

So far they had found no trace of Harrison or Aimesley in this town, which was called Kinsey. The
storekeepers might easily have forgotten them and
wouldn't have known their names anyway, but the
bank tellers would. Harrison had stopped at all the
small towns on his way so far—which Raider felt
was a sure sign of an Easterner bored silly on a cattle
drive—and if he hadn't stopped in Kinsey, maybe it
was because he hadn't come this way.

Raider was outside the bank. Earlier he had noticed that Cal's horse had developed a slight limp in
its right foreleg. Standing next to the horse's
shoulder, with his back toward its head, he lifted the
horse's right front hoof. As the animal's foreleg bent
backward at the joint, he seized the hoof between his
knees and used the blade tip of his Bowie to remove
a sharp, angular stone from between the metal shoe
and the hoof. Although his head was bent over this
task, he did not fail to notice three men who entered
the bank. There was nothing peculiar about the men,
only the fact that two others waited on their horses,
holding the mounts of the three who had gone inside,
looking up and down the street. They struck Raider
like people in a hurry.

Inside the bank, the three men looked around. The
bank was small—a big room divided across the middle by a counter with a brass rail on it that came head
high. Behind the counter sat a single teller, and off in
a corner at a desk sat the manager or owner or whatever he was. On their side of the counter, there were
two customers, one of whom was carrying a gun.

The three men drew their revolvers and had everybody raise their hands. They ordered the customer with the gun to throw it on the floor. Calvin obeyed. One of the bandits picked it up, and he stayed behind to cover them and the teller, while the other two, after leaping the counter, had a serious talk with the manager which involved poking him in the belly with their gun barrels.

He held up a set of brass keys and led them to a huge freestanding cast-iron safe, ten feet by ten feet across and maybe fifteen deep. The safe was entered by a massive door about seven feet high by four across. The manager turned several of the brass keys in the door and then needed the help of one of the bandits to swing it open. The three of them stepped inside and disappeared from view.

The bandit on guard outside was keeping a close watch on the teller. He had Cal's gun, and he didn't pay much heed to a weedy city type like Phil. But he didn't like the look of the teller and guessed he might have a weapon or an alarm concealed behind that counter.

The robber waved his gun in the teller's direction. "Why don't you climb over that counter and come on this side with us?"

This being the kind of invitation it wouldn't have been wise to refuse, the teller began to move.

"Keep your hands where I can see them!" the robber barked, leveling the barrel of his Colt on the man's head.

Phil Temple's right hand dropped to his coat pocket. The 3¼-inch barrel of his Smith & Wesson Pocket .38 made a bulge in the worsted wool for half a second before he fired. The bullet tore through the cloth, and the flame from the muzzle scorched it. The bandit crumpled on the floor, his unfired weapon clutched loosely now in his lifeless fingers.

A single bound took Cal Lowry to the counter. He

cleared it and the brass rail like a steeplechaser and then charged the door of the safe. He hit the door with his beefy shoulder and forced it closed on the gunman who was emerging. The brass keys hung in the door by one key, and he turned that in its key-hole.

Outside the bank, Raider was keeping busy on the horse's hoof longer than necessary. When he heard the shot inside the bank, he dropped the hoof and went for his gun. The two lookouts pulled their rifles from their saddle sheaths, knowing how townsfolk were apt to grow curious about a gunshot in a bank, in particular the one looking at his horse's hoof right outside the bank.

Raider slammed a bullet into the lower neck of one horseman, a couple of inches below his chin. The man's head fell forward on his chest and he did a slow somersault out of the saddle. The second rifle-man squeezed off a shot at Raider, half concealed behind Cal's horse, and the bullet tore a bloody groove along the horse's buttock, tearing a long shallow line through its hide. The animal, tied to a hitching post, kicked viciously backward at its tormentor. Its huge shoulders lurched sideways and knocked Raider on his ass in the dust.

The mounted lookout lined up his rifle on the fallen man for a fast shot, when the bank door opened and Phil laid two .38 slugs in a deadeye beam that caught the horseman in the chest, the slugs impacting hardly an inch apart. The man was blown out of the saddle, and the five horses bolted down the middle of the town street, backing up the story already circulating around town that something was happening down at the bank.

Raider climbed to his feet, blowing dust from the chambers of his Remington .44. "You're really beginning to get the hang of things, kid," he said to Phil as he followed him into the bank.

The very fact that Raider said anything at all made Phil proud as hell. Phil took Cal's gun from the dead bandit inside, and he and Raider climbed over the counter. Cal was bellowing at the safe door.

"You can't hear much from inside, and I reckon they can't hear me well either," Cal explained, "but here's what I think they want. They'll kill the manager if we keep them locked in there. If we let them out, they'll use him as a hostage till they get clear of town, then let him go. They told me to hurry and open this door before it's too late."

Raider looked around him for a moment, then kicked off his boots, He climbed up the bolts of the safe door and hauled himself quietly up on its roof. He walked softly on the top and nodded to Cal.

Cal turned the key and heaved the door open a few inches.

"Who's there?" a suspicious voice rasped from inside.

"Just us two," Cal answered. "The ones you saw."

"Who's outside the bank?"

"I don't know," Cal said. "I ain't been outside."

"You and the other fella, get in front of the crack so I can see the two of you. Okay. Now back over to that counter and put your guns on the floor. Where I can see them. I ain't taking my eye off of you two, so don't try nothing."

The door very slowly opened outward. One of the gunmen emerged, holding a revolver in his right hand and a heavy, partly filled flour sack in his left. He looked warily about him but not over his head. Next came the manager, hands clasped behind his neck, sweat running down his forehead. The other bandit also held his pistol in his right hand, flour sack in his left.

Raider leaped and hit the last man to emerge square in the back with his stockinged feet. The gunman went down like a ninepin and knocked the bank manager off his feet in front of him. The manager was a bulky man, and he really came down hard on the bandit before him.

They bound the two surviving bandits and handed them over to the townspeople. The bank manager insisted on treating the three Pinkertons to a meal. No, he had not seen Aimesley or Harrison. When they came out of the eating house, the first sight that met their eyes was the two bank robbers strung up from a porch outside the hardware store, their heels barely off the boardwalk.

"I went to the trouble of taking those two alive so they could stand trial," Raider told a group of townspeople.

One man said, "They did get a trial. Twelve men found them guilty."

"Well, we couldn't have taken them with us," Raider said to Phil and Cal. "Damn!" he said and slapped his thigh. "Well, it's too late now."

"What is?"

"I forgot to ask them if they'd seen Harrison or Aimesley."

CHAPTER SEVEN

Bob took the herd by a shortcut which avoided the long way around Kinsey and where there was plenty of water and grass. The white-whiskered prospector was contrary and opinionated—he and the cook had threatened to kill each other several times—but everyone appreciated how his knowledge of the country made the going much easier. Also, it couldn't be denied that he could handle cattle far better than any of the so-called cowpunchers hired for the drive. His latest contrariness was that he was tired of eating beef and sowbelly. He felt like some prairie chicken. These large, brown, henlike birds were plentiful in the grasslands and were often flushed from under their horses' hooves. No one else had complained—in case the cook threw something at him—but something different from fried beef and beans twice a day for weeks on end sounded good.

Cluskey went with Bob to shoot some prairie chickens for the pot. The old prospector had scoffed at the offer of a modern breech-loading shotgun that fired cartridges, taking his old-fashioned side-by-side muzzle-loader. Cluskey had never hit anything with a shotgun except beer bottles tossed in the air, but he figured that his modern double-barrel weapon would more than make up for his lack of experience. Against Bob's venerable fowling piece, Cluskey felt his new gun would make him look like a crack shot.

He watched the sun-dried sourdough pull out the loading rod from under the barrels and then brace the gun, barrels upward, between his knees. Next he took a metal flask labeled DuPont Superfine FFg Gunpowder, Wilmington, Delaware.

"Used to make my own in the old days," he remarked. "Been always the same contents in blackpowder, seventy-five percent saltpeter, fifteen percent charcoal, and ten percent sulfur. This storebought stuff is good quality. The FFg is mediumgrain and burns up faster than the coarse-grain, like Fg. It don't foul up the inside of the barrels so fast either." He poured a quantity of powder into each barrel. "You want to be careful doing this if your gun is still hot from firing. Old pard of mine lost his hand when his flask blew. That didn't hold him back none after a couple of years though. He got a big sharp hook put on. Killed a man with it later in a barroom fight in Baker City."

He fumbled in a pocket and brought out a piece of nitro card cut in a circle to match that of the gun barrels. Having split the nitro card with a fingernail, he dropped a half down each barrel. Next he tipped a flask of birdshot into each barrel and spat down the barrels.

"That's to ease the passage of the shot," he said.

"Only thing is, you're looking down two loaded barrels when you do it. It ain't hard to lose the top of your head."

Bob finished things off by dropping another half nitro card in each barrel, which he pushed tight against the load, using the ramrod.

"I got about equal volumes of shot and black powder in there," he said. "For this twelve gauge, I use about one and a half ounces of shot and four drams of powder. Your hand gets to be the best judge, like a cook throwing salt in the pot."

He searched again in his pocket and came out with a palm of loose caps, tobacco shreds, and plant seeds. He picked out two caps, placed them in his gun, and nodded that he was ready to go.

Cluskey thumbed the lever, broke his shotgun, slipped two cartridges in, and snapped the gun closed. He grinned at Bob.

"That's just a lazy man's way of doing things," the prospector grumbled.

They walked through the long grass and scrub, side by side, guns ready. The first two birds that broke cover, Bob brought down with a single shot. A bit farther on, five birds rose up and Jimmy gave them both barrels. He looked after them in amazement as they flew away.

"I never even ruffled their feathers," he said.

"I reckon they were faulty," Bob volunteered. "Them newfangled cartridges of yours."

Seth McDade picked a steep incline just before the crest of the hill. "They'll be slowed up some by this," he said to his two brothers.

They nodded their assent, and all three rode into the cover of a clump of heavy brush. They tied their horses and squatted down to roll some cigarettes and wait. The stagecoach was due to come by sometime today, and if it didn't come today, for sure it would come tomorrow. They were going nowhere.

One brother shot two jackrabbits and roasted them on a spit over a fire of seasoned old brushwood that gave off little smoke. A few weeks before, while waiting to hold up some silver miners on their way into town, the three McDades had been ambushed themselves by a Bannock war party. They had fought off their attackers with their rifles and hadn't forgotten what had given their presence away—a tall finger of smoke from a cooking fire.

The McDades had lost their father in the war. He had been killed by Sherman's troops outside Columbia, South Carolina, far from his beloved Baton Rouge, Louisiana. His widow had taken her four boys and one girl to East Texas. The girl married, the oldest boy died in a knife fight with a Mexican, typhoid fever finished the widow. The Texas Rangers nearly finished the three remaining boys, because of some rustling, except they had sense enough to throw down their guns and walk out with their hands in the air. Because of their tender years, the judge went easy on them. When they were sprung from jail, they started a new life where nobody knew their names. They picked Colorado first, and after folks there got to know their names, they moved to Wyoming. When things got tight in Wyoming, they tried Idaho.

A train of freight wagons passed on the trail, headed west. The McDades kept out of sight. The stage would be coming east, and they didn't want any warning to be given to the coach driver about suspicious characters waiting along the trail. When the stagecoach did come, it raised a racket that would have woken them up if they had been asleep. It seemed like a mile away they could hear the coach driver hollering at his horses.

"Must be Whispering Johnson," Seth told his brothers. "I hear he don't travel with a guard."

Whispering Johnson it was. They could see his bald head plain and his black beard, hear his cussing and singing and joking with the occupants of the coach, who had no trouble hearing his voice above the rattling and creaking of the vehicle. The brothers pulled their bandannas up over their noses, loosed their horses, and jumped in the saddle. Just before the coach came alongside, they broke from the brush.

Johnson was by himself on the box seat, with no one riding shotgun. The horses were laboring up the slope, with the help of his advice and his whip cracking over their backs without actually touching them. The animals feared the crack of the whip more than its lash, just as they feared his voice more than they did the man.

When the McDades shouted up to Whispering Johnson to halt the coach, he pretended first not to see them and, after that, not to hear what they were saying. By the time Seth had stuck a double-barrel sawed-off shotgun in the side of his face and cleared up all possible confusion between them, the coach had reached the top of the hill and began to roll on the downgrade. Johnson pulled on the lines, yelled to the horses, hauled back on the brake, and raised his hands in the air.

"Throw down the box," Seth commanded.

The coach driver made as if to do so, but instead kicked off the brake and yelled at his leaders. The heavy coach, unchecked by the brake, crowded the wheelers. They in turn crowded the swing team, and all plunged ahead to keep up with the leaders, who were obeying Whispering's renewed yells to go forward.

Seeing that the team would be hard to stop if it built a fast run downhill, Seth McDade emptied one barrel into Whispering's body and tried to kill a wheel horse with the other barrel. The wheel horse fell, but the other five terrified animals dragged him downhill half a mile before the coach capsized and left them in a kicking, struggling tangle.

The McDades galloped up as the four passengers were extricating themselves from the toppled coach. Whispering Johnson's riddled body lay next to the box seat. His famous voice would be heard no more on the Idaho coach lines. The passengers were bruised and scratched, but not badly hurt. The McDades lined the four men up, and one kept them covered while the other two broke open the metal express box. The only things of value to them they found in it were two canvas bags, each containing a hundred dollars in gold coins. Disappointed with this meager haul, they rifled the passengers' baggage and then their pockets.

"Hey, bring 'em round, bring 'em round!" Cluskey hollered, too late or useless anyway because no rider could have held the herd against the grass and water the beeves spied in the lush valley. Cluskey tried to veer the herd away from the farmland, knowing how settlers were willing to die or shed blood for a square inch of grass deeded by the government in their name. A cowhand, used to driving a large herd over limitless tracts of public grazing land, riding from horizon to horizon for a week on end without hardly meeting more than a buzzard, coyote, or bear, was suddenly faced, without notice, by someone sniffing over a finger's-breadth of poor grass. His first impulse was to shoot the coyote. His first thought was that if he did, he would hang.

The settlers saw it otherwise. They had put down roots here, gone to the bother of registering their claims. They saw the drovers at best as exploiters of their grass and water, and at worst as rustlers and horse thieves. They figured that a few stampeded herds and a few dead drovers would get the message across that this land was on the trail to nowhere but bad trouble. The drovers might cuss and threaten, stomp and walk tall, but when they had expensive herds they would run them north or south of troublesome territory, without arguing who had the rights. When a man had a couple of thousand feisty longhorns to chaperon, he couldn't delay to talk terms.

Cluskey and the others had already learned about this firsthand. Anytime they saw settlements ahead, they steered the beasts in a wide berth around them. But tired riders pointing a moving thirsty herd began to think like the cattle they were herding and move in sympathy with them. Often the human rider was just as excited as the longhorns by the sight of a waterhole ahead, and raced them to it before they muddied up the water. A rich swath of green farmland between nude, dusty red mountain spines was sometimes too tempting to both man and beast for them to hold back. In a lust for water and grass, they overran the government-deeded boundaries.

Not that Cluskey gave a shit. He was more worried about ranchers' bullets than federal land grants. And with good reason. If he broke some regulations in driving cows, there was not much chance some representative of the federal government was going to interfere. The big possibility was that a local landowner would put a bullet up his ass. This kind of thing gave a man a real respect for law and order.

Longhorns thought differently, if they thought at all. They weren't all that dumb. They knew their spread of horns, ending in sharp forward-curving points, could move anything between them and water. Cows with calves were mostly murderous. Other than that, they were willing to be unpredictable—easily bullied and just as easily stampeded. It so happened that no one stood between them and this stretch of farmland, and, in spite of Cluskey's yells, no one rode in to head them off.

Cluskey waited for the whoops and hollers, the groans and lamentations, then the bullets of the ranchers whose spreads the herd had overrun. When nothing happened, when the foraging beasts went where they chose and no one came from the fairly closely spaced valley houses to contest their invasion, Cluskey began to wonder.

"It ain't natural," he said to Aimesley.

"A plague," Winthrop said. "A sudden fever could have laid them all low."

Several of the hands were inclined to think it was Indians. They entered the first few houses cautiously, in case they would come across disease-stricken corpses. Every house was empty. Some showed signs of having been abandoned in a hurry. On one spread the horses were stabled without food or water.

"They left in a panic," Cluskey said, staring at a big bed with a real mattress, real blankets, real sheets, and a carved walnut headboard. "It's going to take one mean fucking Indian to stop me sleeping in this tonight."

They hit the valley like locusts. They realized they were harmful parasites, but they were too tired and contented to care. Besides, they had the notion that if a man left behind his possessions in order to flee in fear, someone who scorned this fear had a right to his possessions so long as the danger still threatened.

Close to three thousand longhorns couldn't be hidden. The Indians didn't want them. Cluskey had been told that the Indians preferred to hunt and only ate cattle or sheep in the harshest winter conditions, and usually not even then. His men were armed and had nothing the Indians wanted. They were here today. Tomorrow they would be gone. He and his men were neither an easy mark not a continuing irritant, so there was little motive for the Bannocks to attack. Cluskey was told he could rely on this. More or less. So far as any of the local white men understood. Up until now this philosophy had proved good.

But clearly the valley ranchers presented a different case. They had appropriated traditional Bannock hunting grounds as their own. It was one thing for them to warn off drovers with big herds, but it was another to chase away raiding war parties whose ancestors had roamed these parts since time immemorial. In this case it seemed that it was not the Indians themselves who had won, since nothing was burned or destroyed, but the fear of Indians had been enough. Fear had won. The ranchers, with their wives and children, were cowering in some nearby town.

Harrison, Aimesley, Cluskey, and their hired hands cooked up a storm, slept in clean sheets, shampooed their hair, laundered their clothes, emptied the larders, read the books, played the fiddles and danced in the parlors, drank the liquor, smoked and chawed the tobacco, spat on the rugs, broke some of the windows, and left all the doors open of every ranch house in the valley.

*   *   *

There hadn't been anything even close to trouble for the McDades in Hesterville up until now. The three brothers hadn't bothered the townsfolk, and the townsfolk hadn't bothered them. True, they'd had a few altercations during the weeks they were here, but those were with out-of-towners. Nobody local got hurt. So Seth and his brothers were satisfied that they were well liked and tolerated in Hesterville, which accounted for the shock they got when they were ordered out of two of the town's three saloons, and served drinks in the third only after threatening to shoot the barkeep. That people had disliked them all this time, and were agreeable with them only to avoid trouble, was something the brothers hadn't considered. They never did anything for the sake of avoiding trouble, and had no understanding of those who did.

The death of Whispering Johnson and the wrecking of the stagecoach were the straw that broke Hesterville's back. Johnson had been a champion of the town when the coach line had wanted to leave Hesterville off its run. The company claimed the town did not bring enough business, that the journey was hazardous, and that drivers wouldn't go. Whispering had offered to take a coach through twice a week—and this became Hesterville's only established link with the outer world. Folk could depend on what they needed arriving. They could depend on Whispering.

Now Whispering Johnson was dead, the coach was wrecked, and the company would pull out for sure. The four passengers could not identify the three McDades for certain as their attackers, but they made some remarks, and the brothers could be seen throwing gold pieces on the bar counter to pay for their drinks. It didn't take much genius to make some connections.

"I say it's time this town had a Vigilance Committee," one man said.

"I go right along with that," said another who knew something had to be done about the McDades but was no more anxious than anyone else to be the one to have things out with them.

There was no marshal in the town, and no one even knew the name of the county sheriff. A few locals nailed Whispering Johnson's blood-spattered vest to the door of the stage office and went around town to invite folk to enroll their names in an organization for self-protection. The Vigilance Committee was formed in one of the saloons that now did not serve the McDades.

"Time we were moving on," Seth told his brothers.

"I ain't scared," one brother said.

The other said, "These people in this town are about as dangerous as gophers."

A list of undesirables was drawn up by the vigilantes. Men known to have been bad elsewhere but who so far had been blameless in Hesterville were given a warning. Others were told to leave town by sundown. Some well-known faces around the gaming tables and the dance halls became memories. Notes were pinned on the doors of the hotel rooms of the McDades.

"I reckon those boys ain't able to read," one local wisecracked when the brothers did not leave town by sundown on that day or the next.

"I reckon they're calling our bluff and we make the next call."

"You saying it's time we tied a noose on the end of three lengths of rope?"

"It's too early for that. First we have to take them varmints in."

The three brothers could not miss what was going on around them, yet the longer they stayed and the more hostility they met, the more determined they seemed not to budge from Hesterville. In reality, it was two of them divided against Seth, who had wanted to drift on as soon as things had turned edgy.

"We can't rob no more stages around here, because there ain't none," Seth complained to his brothers. "No one else with more than ten dollars in his pocket will go anywhere without a half dozen of his pards along. Now I want you two to listen and hear this good. You remember our old rustling days? Two fellas in here earlier were talking about a big herd only a few hours west of here. I say we pick up that herd, drive it on east, and earn ourselves some honest money."

"There's only three of us. They could have a dozen or more men."

"Sure," Seth said, "but half of them will be a poor hand with a gun. Besides, some of those no-account critters who got run out of town by the vigilantes are panning for gold down the creek. They'll want to come along."

When they arrived in the valley, after finding that its ranchers had abandoned their holdings to Bannock warriors who had not yet arrived or who had spurned these uninhabited leavings, Cluskey, Harrison, Aimesley, and their riders had at first been careful about what they did. Now they treated things as if they owned and no longer cared for them. What they got for nothing, they could not value.

After they had rested the herd and themselves there for two days, John Harrison motioned for two of the hired hands to follow him. He walked with them to the corral where some of their horses were being kept and opened one of a pair of saddlebags thrown over the top rail. The two cowpunchers saw two bottles of rotgut.

"I want you to help me round up a few head," John said. "It won't take more than a couple of hours, and then the booze is yours. You help me do it fast and there are two more bottles in the other saddlebag for you."

The two men agreed without hesitation. While the three eastern bosses had been taking time away from the cattle drive, supposedly on buying trips, which brought them into towns along the way, few of the men working the herd had seen a drink, a woman, or a playing card since they had been hired. A bottle of rotgut was a mighty temptation. Two bottles were a landslide.

They rode out and rounded up about four hundred head of valley cattle that were easy to gather. Without bothering to put a traveling brand on them, Harrison ordered these beeves run in with the main herd. He could have rounded up more, but he knew it was a mistake to be too greedy. Neither Aimesley nor Cluskey knew anything about this. Which was what made it appeal to Harrison. He wanted no man's thanks or recognition. What he wanted was to be the unseen hand in events.

"Hesterville lies thataway," Bob said. "You need to bring the herd north of the town, through the valley in the direction of them hills."

"It's going to be easy to take a few hours off in town," John Harrison said, "and catch up with the herd again by nightfall."

Bob laughed and scratched his white whiskers. "I ain't seen nothing like you gentlemen afore. I've known men to be on the trail two months without seeing a drink or a woman. You boys get itchy after two or three days. This stopping and starting you're doing is making your men plumb mad at you."

"We pay them and feed them well," Harrison replied. "They have no reason to complain of what their bosses do."

"It's kind of traditional for the trail boss to put up with what he expects his men to put up with," Bob opined. "Your men ain't saying nothing to you because they think you don't know any better. But you can't keep running off and leaving your herd to them. It seems like you don't care much one way or another."

"Maybe we should stick with them," Jimmy Cluskey conceded. "We could push the herd through without stopping from here on."

"I'm going to Hesterville for some fun," Harrison announced firmly. "I didn't come out west to lead a monastic life. If I wanted to live like a monk, I'd have joined a monastery."

Cluskey argued some more with Harrison. As usual, Aimesley was neutral. If they went to town, that was all right with him. If they stayed on the cattle drive, that too was all right with him. Cluskey cursed Aimesley as a spineless jellyfish and said that if Harrison was going to get drunk, by God he was going to also. Aimesley said he might as well go along.

The three McDade brothers and the four drifters they had taken on with a promise of a share in the sale of the cattle hid themselves among the scraggly pines at the top of a hill. They watched the herd advance and waited for it to pass below. Then they would attack.

They saw they really had something here. The huge moving carpet of three thousand longhorns spread over the floor of the wide valley. Since the animals hadn't been driven as hard as they normally were on such drives, owing to the frequent short absences of the bosses, they were in good condition and would nearly all survive the remaining journey to the railroad stockyards. The McDades knew cattle. They saw that this herd was a big prize.

The cows passed beneath the hill on which they were hidden. When Seth was getting ready to give the signal to attack, he noticed three of the thirteen riders driving the herd break away and ride in the direction of Hesterville.

"Hold your horses, men," he said. "Three less gives them ten guns against our seven. This gets better-looking all the time."

They allowed the herd to move on out of the valley where they had hoped to seize control of them. It was more important for them to let the three riders travel out of sight and out of earshot. When they were long gone, Seth gave the order to ride. By this time, the herd had moved to the lower end of the valley and its leaders were passing through a narrow gap cut by a stream.

"Ride up on them real easy," Seth explained. "We don't want to panic the steers and put them running. Those that don't crush themselves to death in that narrow gap will scatter over the hills."

They came up behind the herd as the stragglers were being put through the narrow defile in the hills. The McDade men even helped chase down some ornery beasts who hankered to go by a different route. The cowpunchers eyed them warily, not liking the looks of what they saw. But the strangers made no trouble as they all cleared the gap together and came out on a rolling sagebrush plain.

"We'll pass you on both sides, so we don't cause your herd to veer," Seth offered as the McDade men split into two groups. He led one group, his brothers the other. They knew what to do.

This maneuver didn't make the cowhands feel any easier, but this was open rangeland, and a man had a right to ride where he pleased over it. They said nothing but exchanged tense looks. These strangers were just a shade over-friendly and too considerate too be healthy.

Seth said to the two men with him, "First we take care of the wrangler and his remuda, so they don't have backup horses."

The remuda always ran separate from the herd. Being faster, the horses reached the best grass and water before the cattle. They were moving in a loose bunch, cropping the grass as they went, turning their heads around to look at the new horses on the scene. Seth raised his rifle to his shoulder and shot the horse out from under the wrangler.

"Ain't no need to kill a man, unless you have to," he advised the others, as all three watched the wrangler pick himself up by the side of his downed mount. The remuda bolted across the plain and was already two full miles ahead of the cattle.

Both groups of the McDade boys concentrated now on shooting the horses out from under the cowpunchers. It was no contest. Except for one man who tried to fight back. A McDade drilled him, and the rest got the message real fast. Three of the men dismounted and saved their horses by striking them on the rump so they would gallop away. Two made a break for it but were chased down and had their cayuses knocked in the dirt.

Seth McDade even held his Colt barrel to the forehead of the nag pulling the chuck wagon. The animal snapped a shaft as it fell over dead in harness.

CHAPTER EIGHT

"I believe them fellas you're looking for is down at the Jewel of the West right at this moment," the man answered after Raider asked him if he knew of anyone passing through with a big herd.

The Jewel of the West, in Hesterville, was a canvas-roofed box constructed of pine logs. The floor was earth, and mud was stuffed in the chinks between the logs to keep the wind from whistling through the walls. The counter was a set of planks laid across some freight barrels. Narrow benches ran along the walls. Other than those, there was nowhere to sit, no women, no gaming tables. Even Raider, who was not a man ever to complain about a saloon, gaining satisfaction enough from the fact of being in one, didn't think too highly of the Jewel.

The three Pinkertons recognized Winthrop Aimesley straightaway from his photographs. They couldn't spot Harrison and did not tip their hand right off in the hope he would show up. However, it didn't take long for the bar talk to inform them that these men had lost their herd to rustlers. The barkeep looked pointedly at Raider as he said in a loud voice to Aimesley, "If it was my herd that got took, first thing I'd do is hire me some guns. A couple of real professional gunfighters can make buzzard meat out of any rustlers. Though I ain't saying them McDade boys is soft. But there's mean sons of bitches who could handle them for you if the price was right."

Aimesley looked at Raider and quickly averted his eyes. "One of my partners is doing that. He's ridden east to get men together. We two, Cluskey and I, don't agree with that. We plan to move to the stockyards and alert the authorities. When the rustlers arrive, they'll find a welcoming committee there for them."

The barkeep was a kindly man and he gave Aimesley a pitying look. Plainly he saw it as his duty to bring Aimesley into contact with someone who could really help him, such as the big mustachioed gunslinger just down the bar. The barkeep said to Raider, "You think that's going to work out."

Raider shook his head. "No self-respecting stockman is going to deal with rustlers, and no rustlers is dumb enough to show their faces where certain trouble is waiting for them. That herd that was stole will be broken up and sold several times over and be mixed in with other herds and maybe rebranded before a single one of them longhorns sees a stockyard."

Aimesley looked dismayed. He introduced himself and his partner Cluskey, then related what had happened. "I can't blame any of our men," he finished by saying. "One died. The others were left standing in the grass miles from anywhere, while the three of us drank here in town. I suppose it's a miracle something like this didn't happen to us before."

"You said your other partner has ridden ahead to bring some guns together," Raider prompted.

"That's right. I don't know where he went exactly. From what you've been saying, you would obviously agree with him. Jimmy and I hope to settle it in a more law-abiding way."

Raider said nothing and looked Cluskey over. He was wondering if this Cluskey was tied in with the rustlers. The young man was shabbily dressed, his boots were scuffed, and his gun looked worn down and old. His shabbiness was all the more noticeable because of Aimesley's expensive tooled leather boots and gunbelt, his buckskin jacket, and his fancy, bone-handled gun. Raider could tell at a glance that Aimesley was not going to be troublesome. Cluskey might try something. He had lured the two rich boys out here, made them spend big money, and now they had lost their herd. He might not be willing to let them off the hook now.

Normally concealing his identity as a Pinkerton operative as long as possible, Raider decided that this time he had no choice but to say who he was and what he had come for. He introduced Cal and Phil and first of all said *they* were Pinkertons.

"You don't seem the sort," Cluskey said to Raider, "to hang out with Pinkertons unless you was one too. Why are you telling us who you are? You offering to go after the rustlers for us?"

"Yeah, I'm a Pinkerton too," Raider said. "But we ain't accepting any new jobs right now until we complete the one we're on."

"Who are you chasing?" Aimesley asked with interest, adding, "If you don't mind my asking."

"Two runaway kids," Raider said. "Their parents back east hired us to bring them back."

"Kids?" Aimesley asked, surprised. "They made it this far west?"

Raider laughed. He reached in his pocket for some photographs, selected one of Aimesley, posed stiffly with his father, and tossed it along the bar to him.

Aimesley still didn't catch on. He stared at the photograph in amazement. "Where did you get this?"

"Your father gave it to him," Cluskey said.

"I've never met your father," Raider said. "But it's true that me and my two fellow Pinkertons here have come by to collect you, Mr. Aimesley, and your pard Harrison. Now that we've caught you, we can search for him. Let's go."

Aimesley just stood at the bar, too stunned to say or do anything.

Cluskey spoke up. "We've got twenty-five thousand dollars' worth of longhorns out there. You can't ask us to just walk away and leave them."

"No one's asking you anything," Raider growled. "You're being left behind."

"That's our herd!" Cluskey shouted. "The three of us put it together. No one's going to part us from it."

"You've already been parted from it," Raider observed drily. He turned to Aimesley. "Time to go, fella."

Cluskey stood between them. He tried to catch Raider by the right arm. The big Pinkerton moved back a half pace, then drove a right uppercut beneath the shabby young man's chin. Cluskey was lifted off his feet, sailed across the barroom, and landed on his back on the sawdust floor. He lay spread-eagled, without moving, totally unconscious.

"Like I said," Raider murmured in an easy voice to Aimesley, "time to go."

Aimesley pulled himself together. "You shouldn't have done that," he said angrily. "Jimmy is a decent sort. I think he's right in saying you should not force Harrison and me to lose our twenty-five thousand. Certainly my father is not going to be pleased if I come back twelve and a half thousand poorer on this deal just because of your hurry."

Raider could see the logic of this. He poured himself a glass of rotgut and asked, "What's Cluskey's cut in your deal?"

"When we sell the cows, Harrison and I first get back the original price of the animals plus all our expenses. Then we divide whatever profit is left three ways."

"Sounds fair enough," Raider commented. "Suppose we help you get your herd back, what then?"

"Help us sell it. After that Harrison and I will return willingly to New York with you."

"You got a deal. First we find the herd. Them steers are going to be easier to locate then Harrison. If we have them, he'll come to us."

Cluskey by now was sitting on the floor, looking groggily around him.

Raider jerked his thumb toward Cluskey and said to Aimesley, "Better get your pard on his feet. Soon as we finish this bottle, we're gonna ride out."

Two of the cowhands couldn't be found.

"They must be somewhere close," Cluskey said, "because they haven't been paid off."

"Leave word for them to catch up with us," Raider said. "We can't wait for anyone."

One of the cowpunchers rode alongside. "The fellas asked me to talk for them. We seen the kind of shooting these McDades can do, and none of us reckon we want to trade fire with them."

"No one here in Hesterville would hire out with us

against the McDades," Cluskey said. "That's why
Harrison moved to another town to round up more
guns."

"We ain't yellow," the cowpuncher went on, "but
we're cowboys and not gunsels. The McDades hired
some troublemakers who were run out of town. We
outnumber them, and maybe that makes you feel
good. It don't make us feel good. When they start
throwing lead at us, some of us is going to ride for
the hills."

"Then you better keep riding," Raider told him,
"'cause if you come back later you might get shot
kind of accidental."

"Any man who deserts now won't collect any
pay," Cluskey threatened.

The cowpuncher who was spokesman for the
others dropped back and talked with them. Some of
them were plenty scared of the McDades, and it was
a case of fear contesting greed for the money due
them. Although they kept riding, Raider knew there
was no way he could depend on them if things got
hot.

Bob, the prospector, waved his old muzzle-load-
ing shotgun and swore he could be counted on. "The
McDades have a climb ahead of them today. I rode
out myself yesterday to spy on them. They're taking
the herd over the Coyote Hills, instead of around the
south of them. It'll be slow hard work up the slope
for the cows. Only thing is, they'll be able to shoot
down at us if we're below them."

"We won't be," Raider said. "Show us the southern way around. We'll climb from the other side and
meet them."

They kept up a fast pace and made good time.
The hard riding kept the cowpunchers' minds off
their worries. On the far side of the spine of hills,
they began to climb the sagebrush-covered slope at

a point Bob reckoned about opposite to the herd. Now they had to reach the crest of the ridge before the longhorns. If they didn't, they might meet three thousand steers coming downhill headlong against them.

The Coyote Hills were higher than they looked. The incline was never steep, but the constant uphill work began to tell on the horses, and their pace slowed. Every time they came over a rise and thought that this for sure must be the top, another slope came into sight above them; and after they had climbed that, yet another stretch of hillside was revealed. Finally they made it to the crest of the ridge and anxiously peered down the other side.

The cows were laboriously and unwillingly clambering up its slope, more than two-thirds of the way up. They kicked up a huge roil of dust and caused small stone falls and landslides behind them. Shouting and cursing, the McDades and their men drove the tired beasts ahead of them. Two men rode point at either side, to stop the steers from spreading to the sides and turning back. Those behind the herd rode from side to side, cracking bullwhips. The pace was slow, and they had a long way to go yet.

Raider dismounted and sent the others back out of sight while he studied the lay of the land. He was not someone who spent overlong plotting or worrying, knowing that things never work out exactly as planned. Now was as good a time to do it as any, and the left side was as good as the right. He walked back to the others, remounted, and gave his instructions. They came over the top side by side and plunged downhill, bearing to their left, toward the two men riding point on that side.

Because of the dust and constant effort, none of the men herding the cattle saw the line of riders approach from above. But the longhorns did and they balked. This only made the McDade men work harder in driving them and caused them to be further blinded by sweat and dust. The cowpunchers in Raider's line grew more daring and aggressive as they saw that none of the McDades were firing on them and that the big Pinkerton's plan was probably going to work. At Raider's signal, they all charged downward, waving their hats and yelling blue murder.

The longhorns, driven from behind and threatened from above on the southern end, broke sideways to the north. The leading animals on that side overran the two riders. Hundreds of hooves ground both the men and horses into the dirt, trampling them until they were no more than bloody skinfuls of shattered bones.

Then the cattle did the next easiest thing—they charged downhill. The horses of the riders behind the herd twisted around and tried to outrun the massive wave of living flesh and clashing horns behind them. All survived, except for one that broke a foreleg in a gopher hole and couldn't keep up the pace on three legs. The other horses, although they sometimes fell or skidded out of control downhill on their haunches, neighing with fright, managed to stagger to their feet again in time and gallop panic-stricken down the slope, only yards ahead of the first row of wide, pointed horns and sharp, merciless hooves.

The men on the horses' backs were not so lucky. Thrown from the saddle, one of the McDade brothers and another man were cut to pieces by the heavy, stampeding beeves, their limbs ripped off their torsos and their innards twisted around the legs of the cattle.

* * *

It was long past sundown before they gathered the herd, and every man had to spend all night in the saddle to control the steers and keep guard against a sneak attack. At first light, they buried the remains of the men killed by the cattle, putting them all in a single grave, which they topped with large stones to keep off scavengers. Aimesley had been insistent on this, and even read from his pocket Bible as the dirt was thrown over the mangled remains. The cattle, hungry and thirsty, complained at the delays, for there was nothing for them to eat or drink on the parched stony ground at the base of the hills.

The survivors of the McDade bunch had not tried a revenge attack, and there was no sign of them this morning.

"They can't go back to Hesterville, and there ain't another town inside a two days' ride from here," Bob said. "Maybe they've had themselves an early start, but I don't know. I never came across these McDades before the day they shot us up. All the same, from what I been hearing of them, they ain't going to back off fast and agree to be beaten."

Raider shrugged, like this had no importance to him. "The hands tell me the cows are too beat to take on that hill again without rest and water. What's it like around the southern end of the hills?"

Bob grinned. "You ain't gonna let the McDades do to us what we did to them? My bet is they're waiting and watching right now, hoping we push the cows up that hill. There's a creek between here and the way around the Coyotes. Ain't much water in it and ain't much grass, but there's enough to keep them longhorns on their feet. Other side of the hills, there's good grass and plenty of water."

Raider said little. He knew that the cowhands'

present confident mood was a shaky thing. The herd's lead animals were in a contrary mood, breaking this way and that. Part of the remuda had been lost in the downhill run, and the wrangler needed one hand to help him manage the unruly horses today. They had taken back the herd from the McDades, but Raider had a strong feeling the battle wasn't over yet.

John Harrison was not carrying a great deal of money when he was stopped by six men. He gave them the fifty-seven dollars in his pocket after throwing his gun in the dirt. He gave none of them any cause to shoot him, and they were about to ride off when he told them he knew how they could make big money. That kind of talk interested them, as well as making them suspicious.

After he had told them about the McDades, he said, "Aimesley and I will pay you five hundred each in gold coin for getting our herd back for us."

"Six hundred."

"Done."

That thirty-six hundred dollars would cut deeply into their expected profits, but Harrison figured it was better to do that than have nothing at all.

"This don't mean you get your fifty-seven dollars back," the leader of the road agents said.

Harrison laughed, dismounted, and scooped up his gun.

The leader's name was Nick, who said he was Texas-born and sure looked and sounded the part. Harrison decided he was an all-round hard man, without any bluff. Nick rode straight-backed, like a soldier, and his frame was wiry and spare. His suit was Confederate gray, with Mexican spring-bottom, open-sided trousers and a short bolero. Beneath his gunbelt, a crimson sash circled his waist. His big

black hat was stiff and had a very broad brim. And
Nick had a face to go with the outfit—white scars
crisscrossing his tanned skin, a narrow mustache
above his thin-lipped mouth, green eyes that glittered
like steel.

Harrison had no trouble believing him when he
said, "We'll take care of your rustlers for you."

The herd needed a rest. Raider decided to keep
driving them on the far side of the Coyote Hills, even
though the McDades hadn't showed. Bob said the
grass and water would run out in a few miles, after
which came a stretch of lava beds. There was no way
the cattle could make it through the lava beds without
water, food, and rest. Raider had no choice but to
make camp as the grass started to thin and creeks
became shallower and scarcer.

There was no attack that night—fortunately, because none of them had slept the night before, standing guard on the cattle. All of them got at least six
hours' sleep, in spite of having to take turns standing
guard. All hands were ready and waiting for a dawn
attack, but the sun crept up out of the east and nothing happened.

"They're in the lava beds ahead of us," Bob
warned. "If I was them, that's what I'd do too. Wait
behind the rocks and pick us off with rifles."

"From what I've heard tell of the McDades,
waiting this long ain't like the kind of thing they
do," Raider disagreed. "Sure, I've heard they could
sit in the shade of a tree all day, waiting to rob the
next man along. But revenge is different. The
longer you wait for a revenge attack, the more you
get to think about it and change your mind. I believe the McDades didn't even wait around. After
we turned the herd on them, they just lit out of
these parts."

Bob spat tobacco juice, staining his white whiskers yellow. "I say we send a man ahead to check behind the rocks where riflemen could lay."

"You just elected yourself, Bob," Raider said. "We couldn't find a better man to do it than you."

Bob muttered at this, but secretly he was flattered by what the Pinkerton said of him. Kit Carson never guided an expedition into the Rockies with more pride than Bob led that herd into the lava beds. All day was spent, under a hot sun, crossing the infertile gray wastes. Nothing much grew here except stunted thornbushes. Some of the cattle cut themselves against sharp rock edges and left trails of their blood on the gray dust. Toward the late afternoon, they came to a shallow creek about thirty feet wide. The longhorns waded into it, stirred up the bottom, and swallowed down so much of the muddy water that they reduced its flow for a time. Then the hungry animals set about chewing off all the grass from both banks. Even if they had wanted, the men could not have moved them.

So it was that the longhorns paid hardly any heed to the volley of gunfire, which normally would have sent them stampeding wildly.

Prepared as the Pinkertons and the others were for trouble, when the attack came each man had his rifle close by him and dived for cover as bullets sizzled through the air around them. The horsemen veered away when Raider and the others returned their fire. They tried to stampede the cattle, but the truculent beasts only sloshed around in the creek water or looked back at them unmoving except for their jaws chewing the cud.

At a loss what to do, the horsemen milled about and tried not to get shot by the drovers hiding among the rocks.

Raider drew a bead on one of them and was about to squeeze the trigger when Aimesley knocked the carbine to one side, so that the shot went wild.

"It's John!" he yelled. "These aren't the McDades. Hold off with your guns, men. Give me a chance to shout to him."

Finally John Harrison rode slowly forward alone. He laughed when he saw his partners and the familiar cowhands. "We thought you were the McDade bunch. What's wrong with those goddamn cattle? Did you put glue on their hooves? You've made us look like fools."

Nick and the other five men approached. Nick wasted no time on explanations. "You still owe us six hundred each."

"No way," Harrison snapped back.

"That's not the way you were talking to me an hour back," Nick said. "Then you were begging for help. We gave it to you. Now you pay."

"You didn't have to earn it," Harrison said. "I'm not going to pay you for something you didn't have to do."

The argument went on, with Nick looking over the opposition until he came to Raider, who decided him on keeping to peaceable negotiation.

It was Aimesley who broke the deadlock by suggesting that he and Harrison pay the men half of what they were promised, three hundred each. Nick and the others readily agreed. The nearest bank for them to draw the gold was in the town of Carey. Harrison would ride out with them in the morning, pay them off in Carey, and ride back to join the herd.

"Cal, you go with them," Raider ordered.

"What is this?" Harrison wanted to know. "Am I under arrest or something?"

"I wouldn't want you to lose your way," Raider

said. "You're going to have to put up with us until we drop you on your father's doorstep in New York. If you don't want Cal, maybe I'll go along with you."

"Cal will be just fine," Harrison said hurriedly.

CHAPTER NINE

John Harrison, Calvin Lowry, Nick, and Nick's five sidekicks missed the trail to Carey and spent the night sleeping under the stars on an empty stomach. They found a ranch house next morning, in which a nervous rancher and his still more nervous wife were pleased to feed them a free breakfast and point them on their way. Past noon, they hit Carey, which wasn't much of a town really, but to a man who had been riding the lava beds, hills, and scrublands for days, it seemed a glittering metropolis in miniature. There were women, white lightning, cards—which were all a man had a right to ask for this far into the wilderness.

The eight men rode down the main street and drew some sidelong guarded looks. None of the bunch looked like they had come in search of honest work. When they pulled up outside the town bank, people on the boardwalks began to hurry away.

Nick grinned. "So folks don't get themselves ruffled, when I see a bank coming up, I always cross to the other side of the street. Unless of course I aim to rob it."

Cal remembered Raider too usually staying outside the banks while he and Phil went inside to ask questions.

"We'll wait for you in that saloon over yonder," Nick went on. "Don't you forget now, that's three hundred per man. You going to be able to carry all that gold?"

"I'll manage," Harrison said, cheerful considering the fact that he was the one paying. "I guess I'll take out a hundred for myself to have a good time in town. You too, Cal, I'll take out a hundred for you. Necessary expenses. No one will be counting."

Cal knew this was untrue. Aimesley watched over and recorded every penny spent. "Sorry, John. Pinkerton regulations. We can't accept gratuities in any form."

Nick looked at Cal in amazement. "There ain't no Pinkerton regulations in this town. You spend your money, kid. Anyone who talks regulations to you, I'll blast him."

"I suppose I might have a few drinks with you boys," Cal said, "but no money. Anyway John and me gotta be getting back to the herd."

Harrison gave him a strange look before going alone into the bank.

Sitting at a table in the saloon, stocked with bottles of whiskey, gin, and beer, Harrison gave each of the six men three hundred dollars, thirty gold eagles apiece. The men left the piles of coins sitting in front of them on the table, as if daring anyone in town to come take them if they could. Although their eyes bugged at the gold strewn on the table, none of the local men seemed inclined to

accept this challenge. Some local women did, however. They sat on the men's knees, helped them
consume the liquor, and allowed them to insert
gold coins in their persons.

This scene being kind of raunchy for a southern
Illinois ex-farmboy, who happened to have no gold
coins himself, Cal suggested to John that it was time
they should be getting back to the herd.

The first time Cal said this, John just ignored him
and went on trying to retrieve a coin that had fallen
between the breasts, inside the dress, of the woman
on his knee. Second time Cal said it, John told him
to shut up. This got Cal kind of riled—not what he
said but the way he said it. Cal had noticed John's
attitude changing toward him as they neared Carey.
He could understand Nick and the other men not
being too happy to have him along because he was a
Pinkerton. Cal guessed that some of them would
never have imagined that one day they would ride
and drink willingly with a Pinkerton operative. Harrison's attitude he didn't understand. True, John had
been a bit annoyed when Raider appointed Cal as his
watchdog, but he hadn't held it against Cal. At least
not until now.

The third time Cal pushed John on leaving, John
rounded on him and snapped, "Forget it. I'm not
going. Not today. Not tomorrow. Never."

"What do you mean?" Cal asked, genuinely puzzled.

"I'm not going back east. Tell Aimesley to put my
share of the money in my account. I trust him."

"Raider's going to be mad as hell at that."

"That dumb ox can control Aimesley and Cluskey,
but not me," Harrison boasted. "If I go back home,
it'll be when I feel inclined to—not when some
heavy-footed law-enforcement types like you and
Raider try to bring me there."

Nick and the others whooped at this, their veiled antagonism to the Pinkerton now coming into the open. But they were holding back, not taking sides, clearly in the hope of having some fun. Even the women quieted down, sensing trouble ahead. They had good reason to, since they were the ones who sometimes got hurt the most in saloon brawls, although nearly always unintentionally.

"I'm taking you back to the herd," Cal said in as even a voice as he could muster.

"Try it," Harrison told him, pushing the woman off his knee.

Cal carried a peacemaker, Harrison a Starr Army .44. But shooting Harrison would be worse than letting him escape. Cal suspected that John might not hesitate to shoot him. He had heard some ugly stories about him, mostly proved true. Before coming west, Cal had seen several times how, given the opportunity, a mean streak can develop in a man who had been decent before. He reckoned John was one of these. Cal was going to have to take his gun.

"What're you waiting for?" Harrison jeered, winking at Nick.

"I'm giving you and me time to think," Cal said calmly.

"Well, now that you're thinking, why don't you just quit those rotten Pinkertons and come along. I have the cash to set you up. You'll get to be a rich man and raise hell while doing it. I'm not going back east for someone to tell me what to do. Now you don't have to either."

"I ain't saying it's the right thing, how your father hires us Pinkertons to drag you back against your will," Cal explained. "In my orders, it sounded like your pa believed Cluskey was robbing you. Maybe that's what he did believe. I don't know. Way I see it, you come quietly with us and soon as you get home, just light out again. This time the Pinkertons won't come after you because we won't believe your pa."

"You're a fool," Harrison said. "I make you a good offer and, by way of an answer, you deliver a sermon. You want to cut loose out here or not?"

"You two boys can ride along with us," Nick offered. "We can use a couple of extra men."

"I'm a Pinkerton," Cal said simply.

"You're a fool," Harrison added.

"Maybe. But I'm a determined fool, and you're coming back to the herd with me."

The two jumped to their feet and faced each other, Cal moving in close enough to grab John's gun if he tried to draw it. Harrison was six foot two and his chin was at the level of Cal's eyes. But though Harrison was tall, built proportionate, and good-looking, while Cal Lowry was shorter, thick, and ugly, the farmboy's hefty shoulders and muscular arms—developed from farm work as a child—gave him the advantage over the city youth, who had never worked a day in his life before coming west.

Harrison turned quickly sideways to Lowry, putting his left hip toward him and going for his gun, which was now out of Cal's reach. Cal jabbed him hard in the left ribs. This kind of upset Harrison's plans, since the blow was painful and knocked the air out of his lungs. While he was trying to pull himself together, Cal drove his fist into his left eye. It didn't hurt so much, but John couldn't see for shit from either eye—only shapeless yellow things wriggling against a black background, as Lowry belted him some more in the chest. John swung wildly, but his fists connected with nothing. Then he took a solid slug in the gut, and all he wanted to do after that was curl up on the floor and gasp for air. One other thing —ask for help.

"Fellas, I paid you your money," Harrison croaked. "Don't let him do this to me."

Nick and the others only grinned, enjoying the show. If they had any respect for either one, it was for Cal, who had shown he could use his fists. Then one man said two words that suddenly changed everything. He said, "Dirty Pinkerton!"

Bottles crashed and the women screamed as the six men heaved them aside in order to get at the Pinkerton operative. In their blind rage and lust for blood, they had forgotten he was a man named Cal Lowry. All they saw in front of them was a symbol of the feared and hated Pinkerton National Detective Agency. Here was their chance to make a little personal statement about how they felt.

Cal had no chance. He punched one man in the mouth so hard the man's teeth cut his knuckles. He hit another on the side of the head and his fist scraped across the man's ear, almost tearing it off and making him howl like a coyote. But he was taking punches himself—solid blows to the jaw from the cunning and hard-to-hit Nick, who kept his distance until Cal threw a blow at someone else, then connected fast at the unguarded moment.

One shot below the right ear knocked Cal silly. After that, they beat him as they wished. When he fell, they kicked and stomped him until the women forced them away from his unconscious body.

This was when Nick spotted that most of the gold coins had disappeared from the table.

"Grab them bitches!" he yelled. "We been robbed."

* * *

No bones broken, except maybe for a few cracked ribs, Cal Lowry forced himself into the saddle the next day. He had come to in a cell in the town jail. Nick had had him arrested for trying to kidnap Harrison! Cal still had his Pinkerton identity papers on him, so the marshal listened to his story and let him go.

"You say this Harrison ain't wanted for a crime?" the marshal asked.

"No, sir."

"Then I can't throw him in a cell just because you want to bring him home to his daddy. And I can't arrest those other bums because they said they was rescuing him from you, which is fair enough since Harrison ain't a wanted man so far as the law is concerned.

"I understand, sir."

"What you going to do about it, then?"

"Go find myself a big, mean Pinkerton to show them a thing or two."

The marshal laughed and wished him luck. He helped Cal wash off his cuts and bruises before buying him a plate of flapjacks and a cup of coffee.

"Do me a favor, son," he said. "Don't come back to Carey again. I'm tired of burying young fellas like you."

Every step the horse moved, Cal's body ached. But he kept going. After a long while, he hardly felt the pain anymore. It was as if he were outside his own body, aware that it was hurting bad, while he somehow no longer cared. This made Cal nervous. It could mean his soul was getting ready to leave his body, that he was going to die. His had been a strict religious upbringing, yet he had been a bit wild for the last couple of years. He wasn't ready to meet his maker. He needed more time.

In rough shape by the time he reached the herd, Cal was helped off his horse. When Raider had heard his story, he ordered Cal to rest up and told some others to saddle up right away.

"Give me an hour's rest, Raider, and I can go back to Carey with you," Cal pleaded.

Raider slapped his shoulder, which hurt even more than riding the horse, and said to him, "I want you to stay here and watch Aimesley while Phil and I are gone."

"Ain't no use in asking me to watch Aimesley when I already lost Harrison."

Raider shook his head. "Harrison's not lost. You're gonna see him back here in a hurry."

But before Raider rode out, he spoke with Bob. "Cal there is in poor shape and don't know it. Take care of him."

Bob nodded.

"And I don't know what goes on in these rich boys' heads," Raider went on, "but if Aimesley tries anything, give him some birdshot in the ass from that ancient cannon of yours."

"Aimesley ain't the problem. Harrison's the one who's the breakaway critter. You rope and brand him good, and tell him next time you'll cut his balls off."

Raider grinned. "The son of a bitch knows I have to try to return him home in good condition, so he's sure he don't have anything real serious to fear from me. Maybe I'll stand on his face by accident."

"You taking Cluskey with you?"

"Yeah. If he backs Harrison, *his* balls I'll cut for sure."

"You're too hard on him, Raider. Long as I known him, he's been doing his best."

Raider only grunted and moved toward his horse. He, his fellow Pinkerton Phil Temple, Jimmy Cluskey, and two cowhands set out for Carey, about two hours' fast ride away. Ten dollars in extra pay and the lure of a few hours in a town had been enough to overcome the cowhands' shyness of gunplay.

Jimmy Cluskey was surprised when Raider asked him to go along. Ever since he had picked himself up from the floor of a saloon called the Jewel of the West, in Hesterville, after Raider put him there with a single punch, Jimmy had been quick to obey the big Pinkerton's orders. Having grown up on the streets of New York, Jimmy was accustomed to being agreeable to anyone who could floor him with one blow. He didn't question the justice of it all—he just tried to keep from being hit too often.

But that didn't mean he had to kowtow or kiss ass. Cluskey had a way of letting someone stronger than him know he would go along with things only so far. Push him too far and, win or lose, he'd fight again. Raider had left him alone after this, in fact had avoided him as much as possible. This was why he was surprised to be included by Raider in the party headed for Carey. All three of the Pinkertons seemed to look on him as the instigator of this whole thing out west. But he saw no reason to admit it to them.

There was no reason for Jimmy to give the three Pinkertons any friction. Why should he? They hadn't come for him. They were working as three unpaid hands to help drive the herd. With Raider along, they had a lot less to fear from rustlers and so forth farther along. The Pinkertons weren't going to interfere with him getting his share; in fact, having the Pinkertons along was a sort of insurance he would get it. Finally, Raider might straighten out Harrison. Jimmy doubted it. Yet if anyone could, it was Raider. John had been fairly quiet since the Pinkertons had joined them. Now things had come to a boil with him again.

They reached Carey, with nothing much happening on the way. In the first saloon they entered in the town, they recognized one of Nick's sidekicks. He knew who they were too and why they were there. Being alone and thinking maybe they hadn't spotted him, he eased along one wall toward the door.

"Hey there, pard!" Raider's voice boomed at him and made him jump. "Come over here and help us kill a bottle of rotgut."

"I'd like to but I gotta be going," the fella mumbled and tried to slide outside.

The fingers of Raider's right hand dug into his shoulder in an iron grip and hauled him back inside. "You don't want to hurt our feelings by not having a drink with us."

The man agreed that he didn't want to hurt their feelings and would have a drink with them to avoid causing them pain. He had several very fast drinks almost poured into him by Raider. When the Pinkerton ordered a second bottle, the man again tried to leave. Raider kind of misstepped, like a drunk would do, staggered, and trapped the man against the bar with his full weight. It was only for a few seconds, but the man groaned like a redwood had fallen on him. Raider forced some more drinks on him to help him recover.

"We're looking for our pard Harrison," the Pinkerton said pleasantly when he judged Nick's sidekick could talk again.

"I guessed you were."

"Where is he?"

"Dunno."

Raider picked up the whiskey bottle, looked at its label a moment, then put it down heavily on the bar on top of the man's right hand. Some of the narrow fragile bones between the wrist and knuckles crackled a bit if they didn't break. The Pinkerton had to wait a spell before asking his next question, because Nick's friend was doubled over, nursing his hand in one armpit. But he was starting to get the drift of Raider's conversation.

"Where's Harrison?"

"Don't hit me."

"I didn't hit you." Raider's voice was that of someone unjustly accused. "I don't care about Nick or any of you. I want Harrison. Give him to me."

"He's here in town. Maybe in one of the saloons or the whorehouse or the hotel." The man moved the fingers of his crushed right hand, grimaced with pain, and reached for the whiskey bottle.

Raider was thinking satisfied thoughts about this hombre's gun hand being of no real use to him for a day or two, and so he was a little careless. The dude grabbed the bottle by its neck and swung it hard against Raider's forehead. The glass shattered, and blood streamed down Raider's face. But the Pinkerton's expression did not change. He never blinked, he did not move a muscle—only stared at the man who had hit him. This kind of unnerved the dude, who was left holding the bottle neck with attached daggerlike slivers of glass. These he jabbed at Raider's eyes.

Raider suddenly came to life. He jerked his head back out of range of the glass slivers and caught the man's right wrist from underneath. Pinning him against the bar, the Pinkerton forced the shattered bottle neck back toward the man's own face. He dropped it when the razor edge was a few inches from his nose.

Holding on to his wrist with both hands, Raider beat him against the bar a couple of times, like he was trying to knock dust out of him.

Before he left the saloon, Raider said to the motionless supine figure on the floor, "Tell Nick I'm in town."

The man gave no sign he was able to hear.

Raider made the rounds alone. The others went in pairs, Phil with one cowhand, Cluskey with the other. They tried the saloons, the whorehouse, the hotel, the stores. Harrison was not to be found, and no one admitted having seen him, which of course meant nothing. Raider was mostly keeping an eye on the two livery stables near each other on the same street. He was thinking that Harrison might cut and run when he heard they were in town. He might already have gone.

Raider's challenge to Nick by way of his damaged sidekick had not been mere bravado. He wanted to keep Nick in town, figuring from Cal's story that Harrison was with him still. If there was one way to keep a proud son of a gun like Nick in town, that way was to make threats or taunts about him. If he left town then, it would look like he was running away. For a man like Nick, his name meant everything to him. He would go to any length to make sure there was no misunderstanding on that score. Raider knew this outlook very well, having a lot of it himself. If Nick stayed, chances were Harrison would too.

"You been careful?" Raider asked the others when they got together after their fruitless search. He had warned them that Nick's obvious revenge was to beat up on one or two of them—or worse.

"We've been careful," Phil said. "We've been discussing something, Raider. All of us were down the bar a ways when that varmint hit you with the bottle. We didn't want to make it look like a bunch of us were ganging up on a lone man. We were too far to stop him from hitting you, but we did see the look on your face. Cluskey wants to know how you learn to take a bottle blow on the head without scrunching up your face."

"It takes years of practice," Raider said without cracking a smile. "That was my dumb look. I saw the bottle coming, but I saw it too late to move my head out of the way. So I tried to be dignified about it. That's the way I reckon I'll go someday when that bullet with my name on it starts heading my way."

They all looked very impressed by this. Then they split up to search around town again. Phil hurried back in a little while with word that Nick was gunning for Raider. An agitated Cluskey came not long after, saying Nick was giving Raider a full hour to leave town. Still no sign of John Harrison.

Raider seemed relieved. "Good. That gives me just enough time to do something very important. If you boys want to tag along, I'm going now."

The four stuck close with him, curious to know what this important thing was. They guessed it was some Pinkerton technique which would lay Nick low. When Raider went in the whorehouse, they began to have second thoughts.

Raider left the others to do whatever they wanted to do. He saw a big redhead that took his fancy straightaway. She was sitting in her underclothes, smoking a cigarette, and playing with a long necklace. She was the kind of powerful vision that can come to a lonely rider too long on the trail, except she was flesh-and-blood real. When he met her gaze and nodded, she rose lazily as a big cat, presented her bottom to him as she stooped to stub out her cigarette, straightened up, and beckoned him to follow her to a back room.

Once they were inside the room, she locked the door and headed behind a dressing screen, over which she threw her clothes as she removed them. Raider kicked off his boots and dropped his clothes on the floor. When she emerged from behind the screen, they stood naked looking at each other. She had a flat stomach and long legs, and a rich, gleaming mound of red hair a shade lighter than that of her head. Her large firm breasts had full moons of dark flesh encircling her nipples. Her shoulders were thin, her cheekbones high, her hair hung in luxuriant curls to her shoulders.

Raider stepped forward and grabbed her around the waist. She wrapped her arms around him and, for one long moment, they embraced, molded to each other. His cock was stiff and hard, pressing against her. Her legs parted, and she ground her pelvis against him. They kissed, and she thrust her tongue deep in his mouth. Suddenly she pulled away.

After doing a few turns around the room so he could admire her body, she approached the bed instead of him. Turning back the sheet with a smile, she spread herself flat and beckoned him.

Raider quickly obliged. He balanced himself on one arm, took one of her nipples in his left hand, and gently massaged it. He then lowered himself and began to kiss one breast as he massaged the other. He sucked and fondled them while reaching down with his right hand beneath her sexual hair. He worked on her slowly, seeking out her crevice with a finger, sliding one in, then another. She moaned softly and sought his mouth with hers.

She lifted a leg in a wide arc to give him better access to her secret parts, then pulled him against her as she rolled onto her side and threw her leg over his waist. He entered her, and they ground against each other, pelvis to pelvis, rocking the bed.

She raked his back with her long fingernails, and the harder he humped her the deeper she dug into him.

He came with a whoop and a holler, pumping his sizable load into her. He felt her tighten her vaginal muscles around his cock as she shuddered into an orgasm that shook them both like an earthquake.

Phil, Cluskey, and the two cowhands were waiting in a saloon down the street for him. Raider asked no questions, but he could see by their satisfied looks that they had grabbed some enjoyment too.

Phil took out his pocket watch and looked at it. "You're twenty minutes past Nick's deadline for you getting out of town."

"Then Nick has hisself a problem, don't he?" Raider asked cheerfully.

"You want us to go look for Harrison again?"

"Naw. If he shows with Nick, you take him to one side, Cluskey. You two boys cover them. Phil stays with me to handle Nick and his men."

Cluskey could see now why he had been brought along. Aimesley was valuable, could not be harmed, and so was left behind. Harrison was the same and so had to be taken to one side when trouble was brewing. Nobody had paid to bring Jimmy Cluskey safe back to New York, so he was expendable. He didn't resent Raider for this attitude. The Pinkerton tried to keep things plain, direct, and simple. Raider was letting him know where he stood with him. At first the Pinkerton would have gunned him down at any justifiable excuse, Cluskey was sure of that. Now Raider was willing to work with him so long as he kept doing things Raider's way. Jimmy had no illusions about what would happen, even now, if he tried standing between the Pinkerton and what he wanted.

The two cowhands, having already got what they had come to town for—a woman and some drinks— were no longer keen to square off against Nick's men. They were happy to hear that all they would have to do was cover Cluskey and Harrison's retreat.

Had it been any other operative besides Raider who had dismissed three men on their side, leaving only two to fight, Phil Temple would have started backing toward the exit. But he knew Raider was paying him a big compliment by not sending him away also. It was an honor for any Pinkerton to be in the field with a legendary operative like Raider. Most of the young Pinkertons Phil knew would have given anything to be Raider's sole backup in a gunfight in Carey, Idaho. Phil would have been just as pleased to leave this honor to someone else.

He didn't know that Raider had guessed these were his real feelings and trusted him as a consequence. Raider wanted no heroes along with him. He preferred to go solo, but if he had to have a partner, he wanted one who looked at the risks and calculated the odds for success. Although Raider's own actions often seemed crazy and reckless to others, things were always balanced by him according to his way of looking at them—and to prove he was nearly always right, he was still alive. There was no better proof than that.

Raider had no wish to fight Nick, and Nick had already shown back at the herd that he didn't want to cross Raider. Neither one had anything to prove to the other—until Raider beat up Nick's sidekick and told him to tell Nick that he was in town. That might not mean much to a regular citizen, but to a gunfighter it was a challenge plain as could be. Nick was sure to make an issue of it, and bring John Harrison along to see what Nick could do for him now that he was a pard.

At sundown, there was still no sign of either Nick or John. Raider warned everyone to hang close together, not to be caught alone—advice for his companions which of course did not apply to him. There were only two vacant rooms at the hotel, and they took them.

Phil brought news. "I paid a waiter for information. He says Nick and his men have rented a cabin at the north end of Union Street. They were still there a couple of hours ago. He said it would be easy to tie horses back of that cabin and leave town unseen during the night."

"Nick ain't going to run," Raider said, stretched on his back on a bed, boots off, hat tipped over his eyes to shade them from the lamplight. "He's going to pull shit on us real soon, but he ain't going to run."

Phil was exasperated by Raider's calm but dared say nothing. On getting the news that Nick was gunning for him, first thing Raider did was get laid. Now he was snoozing on a hotel bed while the rest of them were jumping at their own shadows. Phil couldn't bear to just sit around, and he went downstairs to pace the lobby. He went to the glass doors every now and then and looked up and down the street. The lights inside the hotel were bright enough to illuminate clear across the wide street in front of the building. About the seventh time he went to look out, he was stunned to see John Harrison standing calmly in the middle of the street opposite the hotel, rolling a cigarette.

Phil's first impulse was to rush out and lay hold on him. His Pinkerton training got the better of that impulse. Harrison was the bait in an obvious trap. Anyone who left the hotel and walked into that area of light toward Harrison was an easy mark for a rifleman. Phil pounded up the stairs to Raider's room.

Raider was up, stepping into his riding boots, saying to Cluskey, "I ain't asking you to betray him. You came to town along with us to bring him back to the herd, didn't you? Now all I want you to do is step into that dark alley between the hotel and the billiard hall. He knows your voice. Call him in there."

Cluskey was leaning on the windowsill with both hands, looking down at his partner in the street. "I'll take my chances and go out there and drag him in, if you tell me to, Raider." He turned and faced the big Pinkerton. "But I ain't going to pull a dirty trick on a friend in a dark alley."

He did not flinch when Raider looked as if he might belt him. Instead Raider said in a quiet voice. "I can respect that." He took a rifle from a corner of the room and handed it to Cluskey. "Keep out of sight, keep your mouth shut, and cover us from this window." He nodded to Phil, who followed him downstairs with the two cowhands.

Raider stood a moment in the lobby, looking out through the glass doors into the street. Harrison was lighting the cigarette he had rolled and didn't see him. Raider looked around him and his eye settled on an exhausted muleskinner dozing in an easy chair, his bullwhip on the floor. The Pinkerton walked quickly over, picked up the coiled whip, and headed for the doors.

Harrison was startled to see him. Already the long snake of plaited leather with a length of rawhide at its end was stretching across the darkness toward him. Raider flicked the short handle with his wrist and the thong twisted itself tightly round and round Harrison's neck. His cigarette fell out of his mouth and the next second he was jerked off his feet and dragged face down across the dusty street to the hotel door.

Staying inside the entranceway so as not to make himself a target, Raider unwound the thong from the neck of the choking, crimson-faced youth. He took his Starr pistol and Bowie knife and tucked both weapons in his own belt. Harrison cursed him. Raider split his lips with his knuckles, giving him a taste of his own blood. When Harrison kicked him on the shin, Raider kicked back, making the young man howl with pain.

"You ain't civilized enough to stay indoors with people," Raider told him. "I'm going to make you stay outside with the animals, though it ain't fair to them." He called to a man who was passing in the street with a train of unloaded mules. "My friend here has had too much to drink. I'll pay you twenty dollars for one of them mules if you help me tie him over its back and hitch the mule beneath the light over there."

Twenty dollars was twenty dollars, so the man didn't delay things with stupid questions. Between them they slung the struggling Harrison face down across an animal's back and bound his wrists to his ankles beneath its belly. The mule owner obligingly hitched the beast with its burden beneath the oil lamp Raider indicated. It cost the Pinkerton another five dollars to the hotel desk man to make sure that particular oil lamp was left burning all night.

Raider told him, "Any of the guests get curious about the fella out on that mule, tell them to look up at my window before they go near him. They'll see my rifle barrel."

"Yes, sir." The hotel clerk was not an argumentative man.

"And if that no-good marshal comes by, remind

him that when my pard Cal asked his help, he wanted
to mind his own business. Tell him I sure expect him
to keep doing that now."

"Yes, sir."

Raider went up to his room and looked out the
window. He could see Harrison wriggling on the
mule's back. Having pulled the bed over to the window and propped his back up with pillows, so he had
a good view down into the street, he had Phil set him
up with a whiskey bottle and a jug of bitter black
coffee.

"No need y'all staying up along with me," he
drawled. "I'm gonna be just fine. You boys get some
shut-eye while you can."

"How long are you going to leave him like that?"
Cluskey demanded belligerently.

"Depends how long it takes to get back to the
herd," Raider answered casually.

"That's brutal treatment."

"In your eyes, Cluskey, maybe. Not in mine. If
Harrison keeps snapping at my heels, I ain't even
started on him yet."

"You're trying to break his spirit."

"I'll break more than his spirit. I'll break his arms
and his legs and send him to New York on a
stretcher."

Cluskey exchanged a look with Phil. They knew it
was hopeless asking Raider to relent. They blew out
all the lamps.

The coffee was cold by the time the lamplighter
extinguished the streetlights, with one exception.
Both coffee and whiskey were of bad quality. Raider
mixed one with the other and found they canceled
out each other's bad taste. He had no trouble keeping
awake, either.

It was exactly four o'clock by the alarm clock
next to the bed when he heard a soft footfall beneath

his window, in close to the hotel wall. Harrison had spent an hour sobbing, yelling for help, and struggling, but he was quiet now. Raider eased the tip of the rifle barrel across the windowsill and waited. He had to wait for his target to move into the area of light cast by the single lamp.

If the man tried shooting out the light, Raider intended blasting away with his rifle, which would cause scores of lights to come on in houses along the street. But this didn't happen. As soon as the man stepped into the light, he looked up at Raider's darkened window. Raider recognized him as another of Nick's sidekicks. The man could see that the window was half open, but he couldn't see Raider watching him from inside. He stepped lightly toward the mule, holding a long blade in his hand.

Raider aimed for the lamp-shine on the blade and gently squeezed off a shot. The knife sprang from the man's hand like a thing suddenly come to life and skittered across the road. The man raised his hands high and backed off into the darkness with a scared look on his face.

"My father will sue your goddamn Pinkerton Agency for every cent you rotten bastards possess," Harrison screamed at Raider when he came out at first light.

"Glad to hear you're still alive," Raider said to him in a cheerful voice. He turned to Cluskey, "You see, I told you I'm going to have to break this clown's back before he gets sense."

"You said his legs and arms," Cluskey corrected him.

"Did I? Very well, then. Legs and arms."

Harrison didn't utter another word.

Raider untied the mule and led him toward the stables where their horses and saddles were. The others covered their backs and sides, looking at the rooftops behind false fronts, into alleys, open windows. They needn't have bothered. Nick and four men were waiting for them outside the stables.

"At least the odds are even," Phil said. "Five on five."

"No way," Raider said. "Remember what I told you, Cluskey. Take Harrison. You two men go with them and cover them. Phil and I can handle these fellas. Right, Phil?"

"Sure, Raider." Phil was nearly successful in keeping the tremor out of his voice.

Raider stood still until Cluskey and the others had backed up the street toward the hotel. When he started to move forward again, Nick came to meet him. He was carrying no long gun, so Raider passed his carbine to Phil. "Move to one side. Keep watching the others. Leave Nick to me."

The man in the Confederate gray with the crimson sash beneath his gunbelt fixed Raider with a steady gaze. They were maybe sixty paces apart when he drew his revolver, a fancy Colt Peacemaker with scrollwork and bone handles—not as fancy as Aimesley's shiny plaything, and one that was definitely in use.

At fifty paces, Raider drew his Remington .44. He intended to close in another ten paces and commence to fire. He met Nick's steely gaze and knew that Nick regretted this as much as he did. But no words could heal their differences now. Raider had offered him too many insults. He would have to fight or bow down to this Pinkerton.

Forty paces. Raider stopped and raised the revolver barrel to just below eye level while thumbing back the hammer. Nick's Peacemaker rose in a swift arc. Raider fired. Missed. A bullet sang past his left ear. He fired again. Nick stiffened. Again. Nick doubled over, clutching his gut.

Nick's four sidekicks faded away. The marshal hurried up the street. Another day had dawned in Carey, Idaho.

CHAPTER TEN

There was only one trail boss now, not three. That boss was Raider. There were no more stopovers at towns, no more arguments. The herd and the men driving it moved to the limits of their endurance every day, from sunup to sundown. In a week they covered as much territory as they had in the previous three weeks, even though the land was now wilder and harsher, water and grass scarcer, Indians more plentiful.

"Hey, Raider!" Cal shouted in alarm one morning while it was still hardly light enough to see. He was sitting up in his blankets, next to two cowhands who were still wrapped in theirs and snoring. "Our rifles are gone!"

These three were on the far side of the campfire from the main group of sleeping men. In a minute, everyone was up, checking his belongings. All that was missing were the three rifles. The cook spotted footprints near the fire—moccasin prints!

Cal ran his fingers through the hair on top of his head. "I guess I'm lucky it wasn't lifted."

The men joked and laughed, but they were spooked. To calm them, Raider detailed camp guard duties beginning the next night.

"Pity they didn't take that old blunderbuss of yours, Bob," one man joked. "You ain't got enough hair on your scalp to make you a prize."

All Bob said was, "I've heard of men who weren't scared of Injuns, but so far I've not had the pleasure of their acquaintance."

On the drive that day they saw, or imagined they saw, small bands of Indians in the distance. The Bannocks and Shoshones had fought the U.S. Army and Umatillas. They had been beaten and had broken into small war bands scouring the country.

Bob had some good advice for them. "When a big war party is defeated, like the Bannocks have been, and splits up to travel in small bands through the country, there's only one thing to do. Take that time to pay a visit to some of your cousins who live in town. The change is liable to be good for your health."

"You can forget towns," Raider chimed in, "cousins or no cousins."

Several other mornings they found moccasin tracks close to camp, but never right in it as they had that first time. The chuck wagon seemed to be the main focus of interest for the Indians now, and it had to be hauled in close to the fire. During the day the cook and his wagon, and the wrangler and his remuda, took care to stay bunched in close to the herd. No one needed reminders, and no one dozed on guard duty. The Bannocks were real, and they were very close by.

"So long as they know we're armed and that someone is always on guard," Raider said, "they won't attack. You can be sure they've checked us out and all our possessions. In their arithmetic, one dead or wounded Indian is evened up only by the death of several white men. We're just not worth it to them. They'll leave us alone, so long as we don't present them with an easy chance."

One night panic nearly set in. It wasn't long after dusk, and the night wind was cool and refreshing after the long day's hot toil. Someone saw something move out in the darkness. Others saw them. Figures moving. One seemed to be waving a blanket or signaling.

"Hold your fire," Raider warned. "Ain't no more cause for them to come after us now than any time before, unless we provoke them."

No one got much sleep that night. At first light, they saw the line of stunted trees that the wind had been stirring. The "blanket" was a branch with many leaves.

They no longer dared to send riders ahead to scout the land for the easiest trails. A lone rider or even a pair would have been suicide. The result was that they sometimes came on things unexpectedly and couldn't stop the herd in time. This was why they ran the three thousand longhorns through the single street of one small town, leaving it dung-strewn and in shambles. When Raider tried to call out an explanation, some of the townsfolk shot at him. There was nothing to do but keep going.

One afternoon the herd veered away from something that was ahead. It was a covered wagon, of the kind seen everywhere crossing the country only a few years ago, and now seen scarcely at all since the railroad spanned the continent. There were no horses, and the wagon looked lonely and weird abandoned in the middle of nowhere. Raider could understand why the cattle had been spooked by it.

Cluskey and he rode toward it to investigate, more than half expecting to find the massacred remains of some foolhardy settlers. They were surprised when a man and a woman and two children emerged from beneath the canvas.

"My horses bolted a couple of days ago and left us stranded here," the man said. "I reckoned we'd best stay put till someone happened by."

"You might have been waiting a couple of years," Raider said.

"The Lord provides," the woman said piously.

"I guess someone has to be looking out for you," Raider allowed, none too piously. "You seen any Indians around?"

They shook their heads.

"I bet they seen you," Raider said. "They must have figured you have some very powerful medicine protecting you for you to travel alone like this. Maybe that scared them off. We'll give you a pair of horses and take you east along with us to Fort Hall."

"I'm going north," the man said.

"The Bannocks will kill you for sure. There's nothing up there but wild country, no towns, no settlements."

"I'll find me a lovely river valley where the best land ain't already been snapped up and do some farming there. I appreciate your kind offer of two horses, mister, but I insist on paying for them."

"You understand the risks you're running?" Raider asked.

"I do," the man said.

"I don't think so," Raider countered.

"The Lord provides," the woman said again.

They traded two horses for a bag of cornmeal and

some sugar and helped them hitch the animals to the wagon. Being cow ponies broken only to the saddle, the animals tried to go in every direction except forward. The strange pull of the harness and weight of the wagon frightened them, and they reared and strained against the traces.

"Going to be an interesting couple of days before them horses settle down," Raider said to Cluskey as they rode away. "If he sets them loose to graze tonight, he ain't going to find hide nor hair of them in the morning."

"Why didn't you force them to go along with us?" Cluskey wanted to know. "It's like condemning them to death to let them wander north like this. You know that as well as I do."

"I don't know that. You been out west a couple of months, Cluskey, so you know everything. I been here long enough to say I know nothing. You and me could pass by here in five years' time and maybe some warrior would ride by with that man's scalp on his belt, with his wife a squaw, and those two kids growing up talking Bannock or Shoshone. Or maybe he'll be the richest man in this country, with farmlands and herds or flocks and a prosperous, happy family. You don't know. I don't know. He don't know. That's why we're all out here. You as well as me."

Cluskey shook his head. "It don't bear too much thinking about."

"So don't." Raider flicked the reins against his horse's neck and moved on.

The very next day Cluskey saw another example of the pioneering spirit. While helping to get the chuck wagon under way in the morning, Bob found a jug of whiskey. Toward the middle of the day the cook missed it. He said he had it there "in case of a medical emergency." By this time Bob was finding it hard to stay in the saddle, so the cook didn't have to look far for the culprit. He tried to shoot Bob, but the chambers of his Colt wouldn't revolve because of rust. Raider took the unfired gun from him and the unfinished jug from Bob.

"What's got into you, Bob?" Raider asked.

"I smell gold."

"You smell whiskey."

Bob laughed. "Hell, no. In my nose, the smell of gold is stronger anytime than the smell of liquor. I reckon I'll be leaving you tonight."

"You'll sober up," Raider said. "I thought I could trust you, Bob."

"I'm an Oregonian," he said proudly. "You can trust an Oregonian with money but not whiskey."

As Raider went back to the drive, he spoke to Cluskey. "You talk with Bob. He means to go."

"He won't even remember what he was saying. Anyway, why go at night?"

"It's prospector's caution, so we can't see which direction he's taking."

Cluskey dropped back and tried to talk Bob out of going. "You yourself said that family with the wagon yesterday was dumb to go north alone."

Bob squinted at him suspiciously. "Who said I was going north?"

"North, south, it doesn't make any difference."

"It sure does, boy. There's pay dirt in only one direction."

"What about the Indians?" Cluskey asked.

"They don't have no use for gold. They ain't crazy like we are."

It was no use. By sundown Bob was sober again, and he was still going. Aimesley paid him off and gave him a hefty bonus, because his knowledge of the country and of longhorns had been a big help. In spite of the cook's violent protestations, they loaded provisions from the chuck wagon on a packhorse for him. He climbed up on his horse named Bob and adjusted the double-barrel muzzle-loader on its strap across his back. Raider made him a parting gift of the unfinished jug of whiskey, and Bob rode off into the night without looking back.

After he had gone, the cook said in a mournful tone, "I kind of miss the son of a bitch already."

John Harrison had sulked for a few days after Raider brought him into camp tied across the back of a mule. The cowhands cracked jokes at his expense, and Raider refused to give him back his pistol. The more he sulked, the harsher Raider was on him, never missing any opportunity to show him who was trail boss and ordering him to do things in a way he would never have used with a hired hand.

Cluskey and Aimesley talked with their friend John. Aimesley said, "You might as well try to intimidate a longhorn with a scowl as try to intimidate Raider. Give it up, John."

Cluskey said, "You've heard how he laid me low first time he set eyes on me, and you've seen how I'm smart enough not to hold it against him. It wouldn't do me any good, even if I did. Raider will draw the line at nothing, John, and you're going to be the loser."

Harrison had more or less arrived at these conclusions on his own and so allowed himself to be persuaded. Next day he was friendly and hardworking. A few days later he had his gun back and the past was forgotten.

In fact Harrison was so much his old self again, he managed to point the herd toward some scattered cattle on grassland they were passing through and sweep them along like so much dust on a broom.

Some ranchmen and settlers followed after them and accused them of rustling. Aimesley offered to settle, but the ranchmen got greedy and made impossible demands. Meanwhile, the herd kept moving, leaving the grassland and going into stony wilderness again. The ranchmen tagged along, making their demands until they gradually dropped astern, owing to their fear of Indians.

The pace was slow as the cattle moved through a grassy valley and paused to graze as they went. The men allowed them to do so, and their own horses as well. Raider was no cattleman, and he was not exactly sure how hard steers could be driven without their losing the flesh off their bones. There was no point in driving a herd so hard he had nothing but a bunch of skeletons to offer the market. But there weren't many real decisions to make. Grass and water were scarce enough so that each time the herd found any, it lingered until it had finished what was there.

Dried streambeds formed coulees along both sides of the valley. As the main body of men passed one steep-sided coulee, they saw a mounted Indian watching them. He was in plain view, not caring who saw him.

Raider took the binoculars Aimesley offered him, looked through them for a spell, took them from his eyes, and said, "I'll be damned."

He gave orders to let the cattle be and bring back all the men into a single bunch around the horses and the chuck wagon.

"You see the bright red square painted on his horse's neck?" Raider asked Cal, who was looking through the binoculars at the Indian. "That sign means he's leading a war party. You can bet there are others in that coulee behind him."

"Why are there white circles around the horse's eyes?" Cal asked.

"So it can see better."

"And the paint handprints high on the horse's flanks?"

"Enemies he's killed in hand-to-hand combat."

"How come we haven't seen any like him before?" Cal asked.

"Because he's not a Bannock or Shoshone. He's a Crow."

"Is that good or bad?"

Raider paused. "I think he's making his mind up about that right now. We'll soon see."

The men were now all solidly grouped behind the cattle, guarding the remuda and the chuck wagon, making a show of their rifles. The group moved slowly past the coulee in which the mounted Indian stood unmoving.

It was almost second nature to the longhorns by now to keep moving, and they continued to do so at their own pace even with no one driving them. The riders followed at a distance behind. Raider knew that the Indians did not want the cattle. They sometimes stampeded a herd on the plains that was driven across their hunting grounds, but even if they stampeded this herd it had nowhere to run but up or down the valley.

"There he is again!" one man shouted and pointed.

The same mounted Indian stood in another coulee exactly as he had done in the last one.

"Don't point your guns," Raider warned. "Just let him be."

At another coulee farther along the valley, the Crow warrior reappeared.

"He's playing cat-and-mouse with us," Raider

said. "He thinks he's the cat, and he wants to find out if we are mice."

Still farther down the valley, as they moved slowly along, the Crow emerged from a coulee between them and the herd. About twenty other mounted warriors followed him out of the coulee, and they turned to face Raider and the others on the valley floor.

"Keep riding," Raider called. "They're only testing our nerve. Keep those rifle barrels pointed at the sky. I don't want a shot fired."

The Crow war party steadily approached. If they kept coming as they were, they would pass within a hundred yards of the white men. Most of the warriors wore war paint. Their horses had feathers tied in their mane or tail, or had a medicine bag tied around their neck. Scalps dangled from reins.

Raider took his horse out several lengths in front of the others to make it clear to the Indians who was their side's leader. To calm his men and establish his control over their actions, Raider spoke to them continuously. "You see the small horizontal lines stacked on the horse's foreleg or across its nose? That tells how many times its owner has counted coup. Those hoofmarks on the horse's rump show how many horse raids the rider has been on. I think the lightning bolts on the flanks and legs are to give the horse speed. Easy now, men. They're still checking us out to see if our nerve holds. It's all only a game, so long as no one makes a dumb move."

The most spectacular of the warriors was one who had painted himself and his horse all over sky blue with white dots.

"I reckon that's snow or hailstones," Raider figured. "Believe me, just hope you never find out."

When the Crow leader drew level with Raider, he

raised his rifle in salute. Raider raised his carbine likewise.

The two groups went their separate ways.

They turned the herd south at Fort Hall, down toward Utah. They sold the longhorns to stockmen north of Ogden and drove them in the cattle pens, where they would be fattened after their long journey. The three partners were pleased with the price they received.

"It's everything you said it'd be, Jimmy," Aimesley told Cluskey, "only a lot harder work."

"I didn't know about that myself," Cluskey answered.

The men were paid off, the horses sold, drinks bought, backs slapped . . . Phil had a train schedule. An eastbound train would stop at Ogden in the morning.

"Watch Harrison like a hawk," Raider told Cal and Phil. "That boy ain't home until we put him on his doorstep."

"We don't trust him nohow, Raider," Cal assured him.

"Maybe the best thing you could do is get him dead drunk so you have to carry him to his hotel room," Raider said, giving them what he considered to be a simple, practical solution.

Raider insisted that Aimesley stay with him. "This is going to be your last night in a western town, Winthrop. So you might as well have a blast. Once you get back east, you're going to have to remember your manners again."

Cluskey tagged along with them, unasked. The night went well. Raider picked the prettiest girl in one house for Aimesley and gave her extra money to be nice to him. Aimesley came back looking like he had just discovered the secret of human flight. An hour later, at his insistence, they had to go back to that house so he could have seconds.

Before turning in for the night, Raider checked with his two fellow Pinkertons. Harrison had been no trouble. He was in his bed, snoring.

In the morning, Harrison was gone.

CHAPTER ELEVEN

John Harrison took the first coach out of Ogden, regardless of where it was going. He had woken before dawn with a bad headache and a dry tongue. At first he had only gone downstairs in the hotel looking for beer or even milk. When he got that far without being discovered, he decided to go all the way. He didn't go back to his room for his bags. Today he was traveling light.

The coach was going north. John bought a ticket as far as Logan. If he didn't like the looks of Logan, he'd buy another ticket to somewhere else. He had plenty of money with him. The presence of his two Pinkerton watchdogs the previous night had insured that he did not throw it away. The capital and profit from the sale of the herd were safely deposited in the bank. He was ready for something new. In fact he was ready for anything except going back home to New York. Once there, he knew he would never escape again. His parents would have him married and established in business before he knew what was happening to him.

John could see the truth about himself now. His will was not strong enough to stand against his father's. Or even his mother's and sisters'. They wanted him to fit conveniently into their social lives. He would never have escaped them on his own, not without Cluskey's urging. Of the three, he now was the one who could not go back. He didn't mind the hardship out west, or the lack of comforts and luxuries he had taken for granted back east. He'd sleep on bare boards anytime if he could cuss, drink, and shoot, instead of on a featherbed and have to wear starched collars, be polite, and work.

He was making his choice, he knew that. Aimesley would go back to the old life and bore people for years with stories about what happened to him in the wild and woolly West. Cluskey would work hard all his life, die a rich man, and leave his money to ungrateful kids who would blow it all. He could even see Cluskey becoming like his own father. Well, that was Cluskey's problem, not his. His problem was Raider.

Harrison sat in the coach and looked out at the irrigated Mormon farmland passing by. He smiled when he thought about it. He was a wanted man— wanted by the Pinkertons. Then he stopped smiling, having realized he wouldn't have a moment of peace until he had dealt with Raider, one way or the other. Cal and Phil didn't count. He could handle them easily enough. Handling Raider was beyond him.

Logan was a tough town, at the top end of the Mormon settlements.

A barkeep told Harrison, "The Saints run this town in the daylight hours, but they go to bed at sundown so they can be up with the sun to dig in their fields."

"Who runs it after dark?"

"There's a whole bunch of mean folk around here who competes for that position. I ain't going to name no names, because they comes in here and I put on a smile quick on my face."

Harrison realized that if the Pinkertons came to Logan looking for him—and they probably would— the first place they would look would be among the lowlives in the saloons and gambling halls. He needed to do something here which they would not expect him to. What?

Having bought a horse and saddle, John decided to take a look around outside town. The water channels which the Mormon farmers used to irrigate their crops ran in a vast network everywhere the land was level. Back east, people called them fanatics and heretics. Here it was hard not to admire the determination with which they had made the desert bloom. He had no great interest himself in breaking his back over growing crops. A big cattle ranch would be more in his line—someplace where he could just ride around and be lord of all he surveyed.

Riding around among the farms and orchards, he heard about a house that was for rent. This got him to thinking. Raider would never find him here. This would be a pleasant place to hide for a month. He decided to take a look at the house. It was on the extensive holdings of a Mormon farmer. The first question the farmer asked Harrison was if he was a Saint. His face looked grim when Harrison said no, but he agreed to rent the house to him for a month all the same, if Harrison liked it.

The house was about a mile distant from the main farmhouse, and the farmer invited him to a meal before he went to see it. He sat at a plain wood table in the kitchen with the farmer's wife and kids. The food was delicious. The house for rent was smaller, almost hidden in an orchard. It was new, and the furniture in it was unused.

Harrison was still playing with the idea of taking the place when he saw a pretty woman riding by. He hailed her and learned that she lived alone not far down the trail. That decided him. He had been wondering what he would do with himself out here alone for a month. It mightn't be so lonely after all.

Not only did Harrison find a pretty woman all alone in the orchards, he also found an inn a few miles from his rented house. The inn was at the base of the foothills and catered not to Mormon farmers but to ranchmen, stockmen, and cowhands who worked in the hilly grasslands. He went there the first night and found it rougher than he expected in this seemingly peaceful agricultural area.

"I seen your face before," one desperado told him.

Harrison for a moment panicked at the thought that the Pinkertons might have put his picture on a wanted poster. Then he realized that this was only done for important criminals. He had been gone less than twenty-four hours anyway, so there wouldn't have been time. The gunslinger kept staring at him none too soberly, and Harrison saw trouble ahead. To steer clear of bad feelings, he began talking with two of the man's pards. They said they owned grassland in the hills where they fattened cattle for resale to shippers in Ogden.

"I sold a herd yesterday to the Milliken brothers," John boasted. "At least they bought most of them, with smaller buyers on the side."

"That's where I saw you!" the first one said. "You had a big herd. More than three thousand. Right?"

"Right."

"You bank the money yet?"

Harrison laughed. "My share of it, sure. Those longhorns weren't all mine."

"Where are your partners now?" one of the others asked.

"Gone back east. I'm staying on. I haven't made up my mind what to do yet. Had a bit of trouble with some Pinkertons, so I thought I'd lie low out here for a while."

It was an outrageous boast, and John was sorry as soon as he had said it. Any of these men would sell him out to the Pinkertons for fifty cents. He had been stupid. Then he noticed that, to the contrary, they were now treating him with new respect. They knew their manners—not one asked why the Pinkertons and he had had trouble with each other. John saw he had gone up quite a number of notches in their estimation.

Finally one of them said, "We got a business here that you might be interested in."

John said warily, "I'm not looking to invest in anything right now."

"This ain't going to cost you a cent. You don't have to lay a penny down."

John smiled. "What's the catch?"

"This ain't no flimflam deal. You told us a bit about yourself and said you had a problem. So happens you and us have something in common. We got a problem too. The cattle shippers won't deal with us."

"Why not?"

The man looked offended. "Did we ask you questions about your problem? No. Let's say the shippers don't like to see our faces and don't want to hear our names. Now you done a big deal with the Milliken brothers and smaller deals with some of the others. Everybody happy about the deals?"

"Sure."

"Good. Where did you bring them cattle from?"

"Mostly from Oregon."

"Shit. That's one hell of a way to make a cow drag its ass. Listen, here's what you say to these shippers when we give you a nice little herd of eight hundred to a thousand animals, all with your trail brand. You say once was enough. From now on you're going to let someone else drive those herds halfway across the world. What you did was ride three days west or north and bought the herd outright."

"Why would someone sell me a herd so close to here?" Harrison asked.

"It's only three days' ride for you, it could be two weeks for the herd. Remember the last two weeks of your drive?"

John had no difficulty in doing that. Raider drove them from dawn to dusk. At times John had felt like one of the longhorns, being driven east to the slaughterhouse. "I can understand how your spirit gives out," he allowed.

"Lot of outfits can't hack the final stages. They got trouble among the men or they're just too plumb weary to care anymore. They ain't going to throw the cattle away, I ain't saying that, but neither are they going to turn down anything that seems to them a decent offer."

John nodded. "So this is how I explain my possession of another herd so soon after the first."

"We can put together about a thousand animals every two or three weeks."

"I have to hire men to drive them, sell them as if they were my own, split the money with you. Where do I find these cattle?"

"We have them here in the hills. There's four of us. We'll give you one-fifth of all profits."

"I don't need the money," Harrison said.

"It's not the money. Like we need you, you need us. You see the three of us in here tonight. Fourth fella will be in later, and he's bigger and meaner than any of us. When we say you're our friend, no Pinkerton is going to bother you."

That sounded like music to Harrison's ears.

Next day he rode up into the hills to see their spread. They had about four hundred cattle there, with a lot of different brands. Harrison guessed they were buying up small bunches skimmed from herds by dishonest drovers. They probably accumulated these for a spell before buying a small herd of rustled cattle, then mixing them all together and selling them off fast. They would tell him some inflated price for the beasts in order to keep his percentage down. If something went wrong, he would be the one left holding the rustled cattle.

In another week or two, they would have a herd together. If he didn't like the looks of things, he could always cut out then. In the meantime, these four would protect him from Raider. The Pinkerton Agency would not leave Raider in Ogden for long if they thought he had split for other parts. In ten days everything would look different. Why didn't he just take off to Oregon—or Nevada, even California? He had spent weeks on horseback, driving reluctant longhorns through rough country. Now all he asked was to stay in one place for a short while. He would also enjoy some home cooking and some lovemaking, which brought into his mind the pretty lady alone in the house down the trail.

At sundown he saddled his horse and rode to see her. When she opened the door to his knock, she

flirted with him as she had done before, but she
wouldn't ask him inside. He playfully pushed her
aside and walked into the house, which was something like his own, only not so new.

"Why do you live alone?" he asked, hoping to
hear a long sad tale, at the end of which he could
offer her sympathy and comfort.

"I have no children."

"Are you married?"

"My husband rented you the house."

"But I ate with his wife and children . . . oh, I forgot, he's a Mormon. How many wives has he?"

"Three."

"You don't all live together as one big happy family?"

She was shocked at this idea. "We women are
friends, more or less, but each of us keeps a separate
household. Our husband divides his time equally
among us. At least he's supposed to. He built the
house you're staying in for his fourth wife, but she
died of a fever before the wedding. I suppose he's
looking around for another one."

"Don't you get jealous?"

"At times."

He asked for a drink and she gave him a mug of
springwater. He didn't like to ask for food, and she
wasn't offering any.

"I think you should leave now," she said.

"Is your husband due?"

"He comes tomorrow."

"So there's no need to hurry," Harrison told her.

"You should go."

"I should. But I won't."

She gave him a worried look. He tried to charm
her with a warm smile. This alarmed her.

She said hurriedly, "I don't want you getting any
wrong ideas. I know you infidels have a low opinion

of our customs and think you're better than we Saints are. My husband is an Elder and a very strict man."

But Harrison had gotten used to another kind of woman in the saloons and whorehouses. Gold pieces could buy what he wanted there. He didn't know what to offer this woman, assuming only that she must be lonely and hungry for physical love. The very fact that she was playing hard to get, as he saw it, only made him hornier for her.

"Your husband is a strict man? Balling three women and looking for a fourth?"

"He does it only to build membership in our church. My shame is that I have given him no children."

"Maybe I'll do the trick for you there," Harrison volunteered gallantly.

She didn't even think this was funny.

He lost his patience, grabbed her, tore her dress. She screamed, and he laughed. While she struggled and tried to kick, bite, and scratch him, he picked her up and went looking for a bed. He threw her down on one, ripped off a petticoat, and stuffed it in her mouth.

CHAPTER TWELVE

Cal Lowry and Phil Temple respected Raider for the way he never cussed them out for losing John Harrison. They didn't try to make excuses, either. They could save those for their reports to headquarters. First thing the three Pinkertons did the morning Harrison went missing was to fan out to the railroad company, the coach lines, and the livery stables in Ogden to pick up a trace of the missing man. They identified themselves as Pinkerton operatives, and in all cases received cooperation. Harrison was handsome, six foot two, an educated Easterner, who wore a black frock coat and striped pants. He would be noticed. Phil picked up his trail. He had bought a coach ticket to Logan.

Their horses and saddles now sold, the three Pinkertons, Aimesley, and Cluskey took the afternoon coach to Logan. They reckoned they were eight hours behind Harrison. The coach reached Logan at dusk. The clerks remembered the tall Easterner there. He had got off the coach with no bags. Phil found the man who had sold him a horse and saddle. Cal and Aimesley searched the hotels, rooming houses, eating houses, streets. Phil and Cluskey tried gambling halls and stores. Raider combed the saloons and brothels. It was late that night before all five agreed that Harrison was no longer in town.

"He could have doubled back on us," Raider said over a drink at the hotel. "He could have ridden that horse back to Ogden and taken a train west from there. Phil, telegraph the railroad and coach lines there first thing tomorrow to send word to you here. They're all on the lookout for him. We might as well stay put in Logan until we hear something definite on his whereabouts. Cal, Phil, I'll leave it to you to sugar-coat some pill for Chicago to swallow."

They nodded. By now, Raider had corrupted them from prim and proper report-makers into near experts at slanting a story to their point of view. Raider regarded this as a big step forward in their role as operatives. Allan Pinkerton would not have agreed with him.

"Aimesley, you homesick?" Raider asked.

Winthrop was still high from his sexual successes of the previous night. His matching tooled leather boots and gunbelt were freshly saddle-soaped, his bone-handled gun with engraved scrollwork was newly silver-polished. "I can't wait to stroll along Broadway once more. Do you think I need a new hat?"

Aimesley bought French champagne, which Raider refused to drink, sticking to rotgut.

"You on for another day of trudging around asking questions, Cluskey?" Raider said. "Now you see what us Pinkertons do when we ain't driving other people's longhorns cross-country for them."

"I'm having a good time," Cluskey said simply, spitting tobacco juice on the floor before he knocked back a tumbler of bubbly.

John Harrison got back to his rented house in the dead of night. He hadn't been able to calm the woman after raping her, and he had left her weeping and incoherent. Back at the house, he lit a storm lantern and led his horse to a patch of trees. He tied the animal there, leaving the bridle and saddle on. Then he found his way back to the house and tried to sleep, with his boots on.

He woke in the full light of day when a shotgun blast stove in a window. Buckshot and fragments of glass flew in all directions inside the small house. John took some cuts on the face and arms. On the cattle drive, with its frequent nocturnal stampede or Indian alarms, he had learned to wake from a deep sleep and be on his feet running in a matter of seconds. This was what saved him now. He was out the back door before the shooter could unload the second cartridge through the empty window frame while he was trapped inside like a rat in a barrel.

He almost reached the trees before the Mormon farmer loosed the second cartridge after him. He took a piece of buckshot in the back, high on his left shoulder, and another in the fleshy part of his right thigh. The force of the hot flying lead and the searing pain knocked him to the ground. He might even have lost consciousness for a second. Next thing he knew, he was on his feet tearing through the trees to his horse. He didn't have to look behind to know that the farmer was pushing another pair of cartridges into the breech of his gun.

Harrison galloped out of the trees to the only place he knew where to go—to his new friends, the rustlers in the hills. They weren't going to be pleased. But Harrison was long accustomed to people being less than pleased with him. He would promise them something to appeal to their greed.

The rider on the saddled horse emerging from the clump of trees where he thought he had his wife's attacker trapped caught the Mormon farmer by surprise. He loosed both barrels, but the fleeting varmint was out of range.

"John Warren," Phil repeated thoughtfully over eggs and steak at breakfast in the eating house on Logan's main street.

"It's him," Cluskey said without hesitation.

Word had been brought to town by Mormon farmers of the stranger who had rented a house the previous day, raped one of the farmer's wives, and run for the hills with a band of rustlers who had been operating there. Few of the local farmers having cattle, apart from some dairy cows, rustlers dealing in steers were not a matter of big resentment—except for the dislike that law-abiding, God-fearing men have for those who flaunt all authority. But dislike is one thing and reaching for a gun is another. Now these rustlers were harboring a stranger who had done a neighbor serious wrong, a man they had known all their lives, a church Elder, married to their sisters and cousins. The time had come to rid their community of these godless men—and visit justice on this stranger who called himself John Warren.

Raider said to Phil and Cal, "You'll have noticed when an amateur uses a false name, he likes to keep his old familiar first name. A John can't imagine being called Dave. I hope this Warren fella ain't him. In case he is, we better get to him before the Mormons do."

* * *

The rustlers' spread in the hills wasn't hard to find. They could hear the rifle fire from miles away. When they got there, they found that about fifty Mormon farmers had ringed the ranch house and were peppering it with rifle bullets. Answering fire came from inside the house.

"You take cover here," Raider ordered Aimesley, Cluskey, and the two Pinkertons. He bellowed at the top of his voice, "Hold your fire, men! I'm going in! Hold your fire!"

This madman, with his right hand raised in an Indian salute of peace, walked his horse slowly toward the besieged house. Thinking at first that the rider was one of them, the Mormon farmers held their fire. The rustlers inside the house did likewise, welcoming anything in a hopeless situation. Also, a pause would give their rifle barrels a chance to cool.

A second horseman followed the first.

Raider glanced over his shoulder in irritation. "Go back, Cluskey. I ordered you to take cover."

"I ain't a Pinkerton, Raider. I don't have to obey your orders. Besides, I'm the one who brought John Harrison out west. I have an obligation to him now."

Raider grunted and said nothing more.

At the ranch house door, Raider dismounted and handed his reins to Cluskey. "Don't get off your horse." The door opened a crack. "Let me see Warren's face before I make a deal."

There was the sound of a scuffle inside, a blow, a cry of pain. Then the door opened about a foot and John Harrison's head was stuck out, clutched by the hair in a big fist.

"That's him," Raider confirmed. The head went back inside and the door closed to a narrow slit. "Did he tell you why these farmers are after him?"

"He says the Pinkertons must've paid them to do it."

"You know these Mormons don't do nobody's bidding except that of their own kind. He raped a farmer's wife last night. Did he tell you that?"

From behind the door, there was the sound of another blow and a cry of pain.

"You hand him over to me," Raider went on, "then these farmers are my problem. At least they'll let you alone."

The door opened and Harrison came flying out, propelled by a boot.

"Get on my horse fast," Raider shouted. He leaped up behind Harrison, nearly causing the horse's legs to collapse. This way he protected Harrison from a back shot. He reached around him and drew his carbine from the saddle sheath.

"Pull your rifle out, Cluskey. Look as mean as you did on the day your were born."

They rode toward the ring of armed farmers.

"All right, brothers," Raider shouted. "Back to the courthouse in Logan. You want to see justice done."

Raider knew the Mormons' great respect for law and order. Without a murmur of protest, they pointed their rifles away and went to fetch their horses.

"Go ahead!" one man called. "We'll catch up with you."

"Only if you can ride faster into the hills than we can," Raider said in a voice loud enough for only Cluskey and the others to hear. "One of you, quick find Harrison a horse."

Cal came with a borrowed mount, and they moved out on the trail in a steady trot. Raider waited until the shoulder of a hill blocked them from view. "Head for the hills, boys!" he yelled.

They were most of the way up a slope before the

Mormons opened fire on them. "Keep riding!" Raider hollered. "Farmers can't shoot for shit!"

Next day they had five hours to wait for an eastbound train in Ogden. They sold their horses and saddles, then decided on one last western-style celebration. This time Raider didn't let either Harrison or Aimesley out of his sight. He even went to the head with Harrison when he wanted to take a leak.

"One false move from you, boy, I'll feed you to those fucking Mormons," he threatened Harrison. "Hanging a man ain't against their beliefs."

John Harrison was quiet, obviously fearing Raider even more than Mormons in Mormon country.

They were changing saloons when they met the farmer whose wife Harrison had raped. He was with six other farmers. They were armed and scowling. One of them began shouting, and in moment a crowd of hundreds had formed.

"What do you want from us?" Raider asked innocently, as if he were puzzled by what was happening.

"Justice," the farmer snapped back.

This one-word reply kind of stung Raider. Truth was, he was feeling guilty about having rescued Harrison the day before. He knew he should have handed him over at the Logan courthouse and that Allan Pinkerton would give him hell for saving Harrison, even though that was Raider's assignment. The Pinkerton National Detective Agency made it clear to their clients that they operated strictly within the law and would help nobody, for any amount of money, to evade justice. Raider had been in the wrong, and he knew it.

"What kind of justice?" Raider asked the farmer, hoping for some sort of settlement.

"The courtroom kind or western kind. Either one is good for me."

"What about a very generous financial settlement?" Raider offered, hating himself as he did so, but seeing it as his duty in rescuing a rich man's son.

The farmer spat in the dirt.

That was an answer Raider understood. He turned to Harrison and gestured at the crowd of hundreds around them. "I can't get you out of this one, kid. Which way do you want it? Courtroom or western?"

John's heart pounded. If he was going to stay out here, he was going to have to rely on his gun. He'd prefer to die fast and be six foot under rather than face living death for years in a jail cell—or spend long hours waiting to be hung.

"Western," he said. His throat was suddenly dry, which made his voice croak. He avoided looking in anybody's eyes.

Raider said in a low menacing voice to the farmer. "I won't interfere if it's a fair fight."

The farmer nodded. He got the message. Also, now that his challenge had been accepted, he felt his first pangs of fear. Rage and determination had carried him this far, almost without rational thought. Now he was facing the enemy, hand to hand, face to face. He was afraid.

The two men squared off in the middle of the wide street. One man measured twenty-five paces between them. The crowd scattered to the side, so people would not be hit with bullets that missed their mark.

"Ready when you are?" the farmer told Harrison in a tight, small voice.

John was the first to go for his gun. The farmer wasn't fast so he had good reason to be fearful and had been a courageous man to make the challenge in the first place. He wasn't fast, but neither was John. All the same, Harrison had a fraction of a second's advantage on him, being the first to start drawing.

Harrison's double-action Starr Army .44 didn't have to be cocked. The farmer had to thumb back the hammer of his Peacemaker. Harrison got off the first shot.

John found the stark terror of mortal combat hard to smother. His mind was clouded by fear. He forgot that the double action of the Starr jerked the barrel slightly to the right as the gun fired. What the gun gained in speed with this newfangled mechanism, it lost in accuracy.

Johns' first shot missed.

The farmer's didn't.

John crumpled on the street. Cluskey and Aimes-ley rushed over to him, shouted his name over and over, turned him on his back.

The right side of his face was stove in by the bullet which had crushed the cheekbone on its way into his brain.

They buried him the next day, with a preacher and flowers. They had four more hours to wait for the eastbound train that day. None of them felt like drinking anymore. They just sat around the hotel lobby, reading newspapers and keeping their minds occupied.

Cluskey approached Raider.

"Go away," Raider said.

Cluskey handed him two sheets of paper.

Raider read them unwillingly. They were letters signed by Cal and Phil, recommending Cluskey as a Pinkerton recruit.

Raider laughed. "I thought you had brains," he said.

Cluskey's face was dead serious. "I thought that if I got a letter from you, too, I would take the train as far as Chicago and just show up on Mr. Pinkerton's doorstep. He could hardly turn me down."

Raider said, "Did you ever consider that a recommendation from me might be enough to have you slung out the door?"

"I'll take my chances on that."

Raider sighed. "Get me a pen, some paper, and ink. I never thought you'd be fool enough to turn Pinkerton, Cluskey. You're a real letdown to me."

But Raider couldn't help showing a small grin.

"Dang it," Raider said at the station, "I have to do something."

"Don't be long," Phil warned. "The train will be here in ten minutes."

"I won't be a moment," Raider promised and hurried from the railroad station.

He hated New York City. The thought of going there was just too much for him.

He never came back.

J.D. HARDIN

**"THE MOST EXCITING
WESTERN WRITER SINCE
LOUIS L'AMOUR"
—JAKE LOGAN**

JAKE LOGAN